Everything is purple but the prose

RIDERS OF THE PURPLE WAGE
(The Hugo-winning short novel)

SPIDERS OF THE PURPLE MAGE

**THE LONG WET PURPLE DREAM
OF RIP VAN WINKLE**
(X-rated as well as purple)

in

PHILIP JOSÉ FARMER

The Purple Book

TOR

A TOM DOHERTY ASSOCIATES BOOK

The Purple Book

This is a work of fiction. All the characters and events portrayed in this book are fictional, and any resemblance to real people or incidents is purely coincidental.

A TOR Book

First TOR printing, August 1982

ISBN: 48-529-8

Cover art by: Howard Chaykin

Acknowledgements:

The parts of this book which were first published are copyright as follows: "The Oogenesis of Bird City," in *Amazing Stories*, © 1970 by Ziff-Davis by Harlan Ellison; "Spiders of the Purple Mage," in *Tales From the Vulgar Unicorn*, © 1980 by Philip Jose Farmer; "The Making of Revelation, Part I," in *After the Fall*, © 1980 by Robert Sheckley; "The Long Wet Purple Dream of Rip van Winkle," in *Puritan*, © 1981 by Puritan Publishing, Inc., as "The Long Wet Dream of Rip van Winkle."

Printed in the United States of America

Distributed by:
Pinnacle Books, Inc.
1430 Broadway
New York, New York 10018

The
Oögenesis
of
Bird City

The President of the U.S.A. sat at the desk of the mayor of Upper Metropolitan Los Angeles, Level 1. There was no question of where the mayor was to sit. Before the office of mayor could be filled, the electorate had to move into the city.

The huge room was filled with U.S. cabinet heads and bureau chiefs, senators, state governors, industrial and educational magnates, union presidents, and several state GIP presidents. Most of them were watching the TV screens covering one part of the curving wall.

Nobody looked through the big window behind the President, even though this gave a view of half of the city. Outside the municipal building, the sky was blue with a few fleecy clouds. The midsummer sun was just past the zenith, yet the breeze was cool; it was 73°F everywhere in the city. Of the 200,000 visitors, at least one-third were collected around tour-guides. Most of the hand-carried football-sized TV cameras of the reporters were focused at that moment on one man.

Government spieler: "Ladies 'n gentlemen, you've been personally conducted through most of this city and you now know almost as much as if you'd stayed home and watched it on TV. You've seen everything but the interior of the houses, the inside of your future homes. You've been amazed at what Uncle Sam, and the state of California, built here, a Utopia, an Emerald City of Oz, with you as the Wizard . . ."

Heckler (a large black woman with an M.A. in Elementary School Electronic Transference): "The houses look more like the eggs that Dorothy used to frighten the Nome King with!"

Spieler (managing to glare and smile at the same time): "Lady, you've been shooting your mouth off so much, you must be an agent for the Anti-Bodies! You didn't take the pauper's oath; you took the peeper's oath!"

Heckler (bridling): "I'll sue you for defamation of character and public ridicule!"

Spieler (running his gaze up and down her whale-like figure): "Sue, sue, sooie! No wonder you're so sensitive about eggs, lady.

There's something ovoid about you!"

The crowd laughed. The President snorted disgustedly and spoke into a disc strapped to his wrist. A man in the crowd, the message relayed through his ear plug, spoke into his wrist transmitter, but the spieler gestured as if to say, "This is my show! Jump in the lake if you don't like it!"

Spieler: "You've seen the artificial lake in the center of the city with the municipal and other buildings around it. The Folk Art Center, the Folk Recreation Center, the hospital, university, research center, and the PANDORA, the people's all-necessities depot of regulated abundance. You've been delighted and amazed with the fairyland of goodies that Uncle Sam, and the State of California, offers you free. Necessities and luxuries, too, since *Luxury Is A Necessity*, to quote the FBC. You want anything—anything! —you go to the PANDORA, press some buttons, and presto! you're rich beyond your dreams!"

Heckler: "When the lid to Pandora's box was opened, all the evils in the world flew out, and . . ."

Spieler: "No interruptions, lady! We're on a strict time schedule . . ."

Heckler: "Why? We're not going anyplace!"

Spieler: "I'll tell you where you can go, lady."

Heckler: "But . . ."

Spieler: "But me no buts, lady! You know, you ought to go on a diet!"

Heckler: (struggling to control her temper): "Don't get personal, big mouth! I'm big, all right, and I got a wallop, too, remember that. Now, Pandora's box . . ."

The spieler made a vulgar remark, at which the crowd laughed. The heckler shouted but could not be heard above the noise.

The President shifted uneasily. Kingbrook, the 82-year-old senator from New York, harumphed and said, "The things they permit nowadays in public media. Really, it's disgusting . . ."

Some of the screens on the wall of the mayor's office showed various parts of the interior of the city. One screen displayed a view from a helicopter flying on the oceanside exterior of Upper Metropolitan LA. It was far enough away to get the entire structure in its camera, including the hundred self-adjusting cylinders that supported the Brobdingnagian plastic cube and the telescoping elevator shafts dangling from the central underbase. Beneath the shadow of box and legs was the central section of the old city and the jagged sprawl of the rest of Los Angeles and surrounding cities.

The President stabbed towards the screen with a cigarette and said, "Screen 24, gentlemen. The dark past below. The misery of a disrupted ant colony. Above it, the bright complex of the future. The chance for everyone to realize the full potentiality as a human being."

Spieler: "Before I conduct you into this house, which is internally just like every other private residence . . ."

Heckler: "Infernally, you mean. They all look just alike on the outside, too."

Spieler: "Lady, you're arousing my righteous wrath. Now, folks, you noticed that all the buildings, municipal and private, are constructed like eggs. This futuristic design was adopted because the egg shape, according to the latest theory, is that of the universe. No corners, all curving, infinity within a confined space, if you follow me."

Heckler: "I don't!"

Spieler: "Take off a little weight, lady, and you'll be in shape to keep up with the rest of us. The ovoid form gives you a feeling of unbounded space yet of security-closeness. When you get inside . . ."

Every house was a great smooth white plastic egg lifted 18.28 meters above the floor of the city by a thick truncated-cone support. (Offscreen commentators explained that 18.18 meters was 20 feet, for the benefit of older viewers who could not adjust to the new system of measurement.) On two sides of the cone were stairs ending at a horizontal door on the lower side of the ovoid. These opened automatically to permit entrance. Also, a door opened in the cone base, and an elevator inside lifted the sick or crippled or, as the spieler put it, "the just plain lazy, everybody's got a guaranteed right to be lazy." The hollow base also housed several electrical carts for transportation around the city.

The President saw Kierson, the Detroit automobile magnate, frown at the carts. The auto industry had shifted entirely from internal combustion motors to electrical and nuclear power ten years ago, and now Kierson saw the doom of these. The President made a mental note to pacify and reassure him on this point later.

Spieler: " . . . *Variety Within Unity*, folks. You've heard a lot about that on FBC, and these houses are an example. In reply to the lady's anxiety about the houses all looking alike, every home owner can paint the outside of his house to express his individuality. Anything goes. From reproductions of Rembrandt to psychedelic dreams to dirty words, if you got the guts. Everything's free, including speech . . ."

Heckler: "They'll look like a bunch of Easter eggs!"

Spieler: "Lady, Uncle Sam *is* The Big Easter Bunny!"

The spieler took the group into the house, and the cameramen went into the atrium, kitchen, and the ten rooms to show the viewers just what the citizens-to-be were getting for nothing.

"For nothing!" Senator Kingbrook growled. "The taxpayers are paying through the nose, through every orifice, with their sweat and blood for this!"

The President said, mildly, "They won't have to in the future, as I'll explain."

"You don't have to explain anything to any of us," Kingbrook said. "We all know all about the economy of abundance versus the economy of scarcity. And about your plans for the transitional stage, which you call ORE, *obverse-reverse* economy, but which I call *schizophrenic horrors in tremens!*"

The President smiled and said, "You'll have your say, Senator."

The men and women in the room were silent for a while as they watched the spieler extol the splendors and virtues of the house with its soundproof walls, the atrium with its pool, the workshop with machinery for crafts, the storeroom, the bedroom-studios, TV in every room, *retractable* and inflatable furniture, air-conditioning, microfilm library, and so on.

Government shill: "This is fabulous! A hell of a lot better than any noisy rat-ridden dump on the ground!"

Spieler (quoting an FBC slogan): "*Happy and free as the birds in the air!* That's why everybody calls this Bird City and why the citizens are known as freebirds! Everything first class! Everything free!"

Heckler: "Except freedom to live where you want to in the type of house you want!"

Spieler: "Lady, unless you're a millionaire,

you won't be able to get a house on the ground that isn't just like every other house. And then you'd have to worry about it being burned down. Lady, you'd gripe if you was hung with a new rope!"

The group went outside where the spieler pointed out that, though they were three hectometers above ground, they had trees and grass in small parks. If they wanted to fish or boat, they could use the lake in the municipal-building area.

Shill: "Man, this is living!"

Spieler: "The dome above the city looks just like the sky outside. The sun is an electronic reproduction; its progress exactly coincides with that of the real sun. Only, you don't have to worry about it getting too cold or too hot in here or about it raining. We even got birds in here."

Heckler: "What about the robins? Come springtime, how're they going to get inside without a pass?"

Spieler: "Lady, you got a big mouth! Whyn't you . . ."

The President rose from his chair. Kingbrook's face was wrinkled, fissured, and folded with old age. The red of his anger made his features look like hot lava on a volcano slope just after an eruption. His rich rumble pushed against the eardrums of those in the room as if they were in a pressure chamber.

"A brave new concentration camp, gentlemen! Fifty billion dollars worth to house

50,000 people! The great bankruptopolis of the future! I estimate it'll cost one trillion dollars just to enclose this state's population in these glorified chicken runs!"

"Not if ORE is put into effect," the President said. He held up his hand to indicate silence and said, "I'd like to hear Guildman, gentlemen. Then we can have our conferences."

Senator Beaucamp of Mississippi muttered, "One trillion dollars! That would house, feed, and educate the entire population of my state for twenty years!"

The President signalled to cut off all screens except the FBC channel. The private network commentators were also speaking, but the federal commentator was the important one. His pitch was being imitated—if reluctantly—by the private networks. Enough pressure and threats had been applied to make them wary of going all-out against the President. Although the mass media had been restrained, the speech of private persons had not been repressed. For one thing, the public needed a safety valve. Occasionally, a private speaker was given a chance to express himself on TV and radio. And so, a cavalry charge of invectives had been and was being hurled at the President. He had been denounced as an ultra-reactionary, a degenerate liberal, a Communist, a Fascist, a vulture, a pig, a Puritan, a pervert, a Hitler, etc., and had been hung *in absentia* so many times that an enterprising manufacturer of effigies had made a small fortune—though taxes made it even smaller.

From cavalry to Calvary, he thought. All charges admitted. All charges denied. I am human, and that takes in everything. Even the accusation of fanaticism. I know that what I'm doing is right, or, at least, the only known way. When the Four Horsemen ride, the countercharge cannot be led by a self-doubter.

The voice of the Great Guildman, as he was pleased to be called, throbbed through the room. Chief FBC commentator, bureau executive, Ph.D. in Mass Communications, G-90 rating, one who spoke with authority, whose personal voltage was turned full-on, who could, some said, have talked God into keeping Adam and Eve in the garden.

" . . . cries out! The people, the suffering earth itself, cry out! The air is poisoned! The water is poisoned! The soil is poisoned! Mankind is poisoned with the excess of his genius for survival! The wide walls of the Earth have become narrowed! Man, swelling like a tumor with uncontrolled growth, kills the body that gave him birth! He is squeezing himself into an insane mold which crushes his life out, crushes all hope for an abundant life, security, peace, quiet, fulfillment, dignity . . ."

The audience, tuning in on forty channels, was well aware of this; he was painting a picture the oils of which had been squeezed from their own pain. And so Guildman did not tarry overlong at these points. He spoke briefly of the dying economy of scarcity, obsolete in the middle 1900's but seeming vigorous, like a sick man with a fatal disease who keeps going on larger and larger shots of drugs and on placebos. Then he splashed bright colors over the canvas of the future.

Guildman went on about the population expansion, automation, the ever-growing permanently depressed class and its riots and insurrections, the ever-decreasing and ever-overburdened taxpayers with their strikes and riots, the Beverly Hills Massacre, the misery, crime, anger, etc.

The President repressed an impulse to squirm. There would be plenty of blacks and grays in The Golden World (the President's own catch-phrase). Utopia could never exist. The structure of human society, in every respect, had a built-in instability, which meant that there would always be a certain amount of suffering and maladjustment. There were always victims of change.

But that could not be helped. And it was a good thing that change was the unchanging characteristic of society. Otherwise, stagnation, rigidity, and loss of hope for improvement would result.

Beaucamp leaned close to the President and said softly, "Plenty of people have pointed out that the economy of abundance eventually means the death of capitalism. You've never commented on this, but you can't keep silent much longer."

"When I do speak," the President said, "I'll point out that EOA also means the death of socialism and communism. Besides, there's nothing sacred in an economic system, except to those who confuse money with religion. Systems are made for man, not vice versa."

Kingbrook rose from his sofa, his bones cracking, and walked stiffly towards the President.

"You've rammed through this project despite the opposition of the majority of tax-payers! You used methods that were not only unconstitutional, sir! I know for a fact that criminal tactics were used, blackmail and intimidation, sir! But you will go no more on your Caesar's road! This project has beggared our once wealthy nation, and we are not going to build any more of your follies! Your grandiose—and wicked—Golden World will be as tarnished as brass, as green as fool's gold, by the time that I am through with you! Don't underestimate me and my colleagues, sir!"

"I know of your plans to impeach me," the President said with a slight smile. "Now, Senators Beaucamp and Kingbrook, and you, Governor Corrigan, would you step into the mayor's apartment? I'd like to have a few words—I hope they're few—with you."

Kingbrook, breathing heavily, said, "My mind is made up, Mr. President. I know what's wrong and what's right for our country. If you have any veiled threats or insidious proposals, make them in public, sir! In this room, before these gentlemen!"

The President looked at the embarrassed faces, the stony, the hostile, the gleeful, and then glanced at his wristwatch. He said, "I only ask five minutes."

He continued, "I'm not slighting any of you. I intend to talk to all of you in groups selected because of relevant subjects. Three to five minutes apiece will let us complete our business before the post-dedication speeches. Gentlemen!" And he turned and strode through the door.

A few seconds passed, and then the three, stiff-faced, stiff-backed, walked in.

"Sit down or stand as you please," the President said.

There was a silence Kingbrook lit a cigar and took a chair. Corrigan hesitated and then sat near Kingbrook. Beaucamp remained standing. The President stood before them.

He said, "You've seen the people who toured this city. They're the prospective citizens. What is their outstanding common characteristic?"

Kingbrook snorted and said something under his breath. Beaucamp glared at him and said, "I didn't hear your words, but I know what you said! Mr. President, I intend to speak loudly and clearly about this arrogant discrimination! I had one of my men run the list of accepted citizens through a computer, and he reports that the citizens will be 100 percent Negro! And 7/8ths are welfares!"

"The other eighth are doctors, technicians, teachers, and other professionals," the President said. "All volunteers. There, by the way, goes the argument that no one will work if he doesn't have to. These people will be living in this city and getting no money for their labor. We had to turn down many volunteers because there was no need for them."

"Especially since the government has been using public funds to brainwash us with the Great-Love-and-Service-for-Humanity campaign for twenty years," Kingbrook said.

"I never heard you making any speeches knocking love or service," the President said. "However, there is another motive which caused so many to offer their services. Money may die out, but the desire for prestige won't. The wish for prestige is at least as old as mankind itself and maybe older."

"I can't believe that no whites asked to live here," Beaucamp said.

"The rule was, first apply, first accepted," the President said. "The whole procedure was computer-run, and the application blanks contained no reference to race."

Corrigan said, "You know that computers have been gimmicked or their operators bribed."

The President said, "I am sure that an investigation would uncover nothing crooked."

"The gyps," Corrigan said, then stopped at

Beaucamp's glare. "I mean, the guaranteed income people, or welfares as we called them when I was a kid, well, the GIP whites will be screaming discrimination."

"The whites could have volunteered," the President said.

Beaucamp's lip was curled. "Somebody spread the word. Of course, that would have nothing to do with lack of Caucasian applications."

Kingbrook rumbled like a volcano preparing to erupt. He said, "What're we arguing about this for? This...Bird City...was built over an all-colored section. So why shouldn't its citizens be colored? Let's stick to the point. You want to build more cities just like this, Mr. President, extend them outwards from this until you have one solid megalopolis on stilts extending from Santa Barbara to Long Beach. But you can't build here or in other states without absolutely bankrupting the country. So you want to get us to back your legislative proposals for your so-called ORE. That is, split the economy of the nation in half. One half will continue operating just as before; that half will be made up of private-enterprise industries and of the taxpayers who own or work for these industries. This half will continue to buy and sell and use money as it has always done.

"But the other half will be composed of GIP's, living in cities like this, and the government will take care of their every need. The government will do this by automating the mines, farms, and industries it now owns or plans on obtaining. It will not use money anywhere in its operations, and the entire process of input-output will be a closed circuit. Everybody in ORE will be GIP personnel, even the federal and state government service, except, of course, that the federal, legislative, and executive branches will maintain their proper jurisdiction."

"That *sounds* great," Corrigan said. "The ultimate result, or so you've *said*, Mr. President, is to relieve the taxpayer of his crushing burden and to give the GIP a position in society in which he will no longer be considered by others as a parasite. It sounds appealing. But there are many of us who aren't fooled by your fine talk."

"I'm not trying to fool anybody," the President said.

Corrigan said, angrily, "It's obvious what the end result will be! When the taxpayer sees the GIP living like a king without turning a hand while he has to work his tail off, he's going to want the same deal. And those who refuse to give up won't have enough money to back their stand because the GIP won't be spending any money. The small businessmen who live off their sales to the GIP will go under. And the larger businesses will, too. Eventually, the businessman and his employees will fold their fiscal and pecuniary tents and go to live in your everything-free cornucopias!

"So, if we're seduced by your beautiful scheme for a half-and-half economy, we'll take the first step into the quicksand. After that, it'll be too late to back out. Down we go!"

"I'd say, *Up we go,*" the President said. "So! It's All-or-None, as far as you're concerned? And you vote for None! Well, gentlemen, over one-half of the nation is saying All because that's the only way to go and they've nothing to lose and everything to gain. If you kill the switchover legislation in Congress, I'll see that the issues are submitted to the people for their yea or nay. But that would take too much time, and time is vital. Time is what I'm buying. Or I should say, trading."

Beaucamp said, "Mister President, you didn't point out the racial composition of the city just to pass the time."

The President began pacing back and forth before them. He said, "The civil rights revolution was born about the same time that you and I, Mr. Beaucamp, were born. Yet, it's still far from achieving its goals. In some aspects, it's regressed. It was tragic that the Negroes began to get the education and political power they needed for advancement just as automation began to bloom. The Negro found that there were only jobs for the professionals and the skilled. The unskilled were shut out. This happened to the untrained white, too, and competition for work between the unskilled white and black became bitter. Bloodily bitter, as the past few years have shown us."

"We know what's been going on, Mr. President," Beaucamp said.

"Yes. Well, it's true isn't it, that the black as a rule, doesn't particularly care to associate or live with the whites? He just wants the same things whites have. But at the present rate of progress, it'll take a hundred years or more before he gets them. In fact, he may never do so if the present economy continues."

Kingbrook rumbled, "The point, Mr. President!"

The President stopped pacing. He looked hard at them and said, "But in an economy of abundance, in this type of city, he—the Negro —will have everything the whites have. He will have a high standard of living, a true democracy, color-free justice. He'll have his own judges, police, legislators. If he doesn't care to, he doesn't ever have to have any personal contact with whites."

Kingbrook's cigar sagged. Beaucamp sucked in his breath. Corrigan jumped up from his chair.

Beaucamp said, "That's ghettoism!"

"Not in the original sense," the President said. "The truth now, Mr. Beaucamp. Don't your people prefer to live with their own kind? Where they'll be free of that shadow, that wall, always between white and colored in this country?"

Beaucamp said, "Not to have to put up with

honkeys! Excuse the expression, sir. It slipped out. You know we would! But . . ."

"No one will be forbidden to live in any community he chooses. There won't be any discrimination on the federal level. Those in the government, military, or Nature rehabilitation service will have equal opportunity. But, given the choice . . ."

The President turned to Kingbrook and Corrigan. "Publicly, you two have always stood for integration. You would have committed political suicide, otherwise. But I know your private opinions. You have also been strong states-righters. No secret about that. So, when the economy of abundance is in full swing, the states will become self-sufficient. They won't depend on federal funds."

"Because there'll be no dependence on money?" Corrigan said. "Because there'll be no money? Because money will be as extinct as the dodo?"

The ridges on Kingbrook's face shifted as if they were the gray backs of an elephant herd milling around to catch a strange scent. He said, "I'm not blasphemous. But now I think I know how Christ felt when tempted by Satan."

He stopped, realizing that he had made a Freudian slip.

"And you're not Christ and I'm not Satan," he said hurriedly. "We're just human beings trying to find a mutually agreeable way out of this mess."

Beaucamp said, "We're horse traders. And the horse is the future. A dream. Or a nightmare."

The President looked at his watch and said, "What about it, Mr. Beaucamp?"

"What can I trade? A dream of an end to contempt, dislike, hatred, treachery, oppression. A dream of the shadow gone, the wall down. Now you offer me abundance, dignity, and joy—if my people stay within the plastic walls."

"I don't know what will develop after the walls of the cities have been built," the President said. "But there is nothing evil about self-segregation, if it's not compulsive. It's done all the time by human beings of every type. If it weren't, you wouldn't have social classes, clubs, etc. And if, after our citizens are given the best in housing and food, luxuries, a free lifelong education, a wide spectrum of recreations, everything within reason, if they still go to Hell, then we might as well give up on the species."

"A man needs incentive; he needs work. By the sweat of his brow . . ." Kingbrook said.

Kingbrook was too old, the President thought. He was half-stone, and the stone thought stone thoughts and spoke stone words. The President looked out the big window. Perhaps it had been a mistake to build such a "futuristic" city. It would be difficult enough for the new citizens to adjust. Perhaps the dome of Bird City should have contained buildings resembling those they now lived in. Later, more radical structures could have been introduced.

As it was, the ovoid shape was supposed to give a sense of security, a feeling of return-to-the-womb and also to suggest a rebirth. Just now, they looked like so many space capsules ready to take off into the blue the moment the button was pressed.

But this city, and those that would be added to it, meant a sharp break with the past, and any break always caused some pain.

He turned when someone coughed behind him. Senator Kingbrook was standing, his hand on his chest. The senator was going to make a speech.

The President looked at his watch and shook his head. Kingbrook smiled as if the smile hurt him, and he dropped his hand.

"It's yes, Mr. President. I'll back you all the way. And the impeachment proceedings will be dropped, of course. But . . ."

"I don't want to be rude," the President said. "But you can save your justifications for your constituents."

Beaucamp said, "I say yes. Only . . ."

"No ifs, ands, or buts."

"No. Only . . ."

"And you, Governor Corrigan?" the President said.

Corrigan said, "All of us are going along with you for reasons that shouldn't be considered—from the viewpoint of ideals. But then, who really ever has? I say yes. But . . ."

"No speeches, please," the President said. He smiled slightly. "Unless I make them. Your motives don't really matter, gentlemen, as long as your decisions are for the good of the American public. Which they are. And for the good of the world, too, because all other nations are going to follow our example. As I said, this means the death of capitalism, but it also means the death of socialism and communism, too."

He looked at his watch again. "I thank you, gentlemen."

They looked as if they would like to continue talking, but they left. There was a delay of a few seconds before the next group entered.

He felt weary, even though he knew that he would win out. The years ahead would be times of trouble, of crises, of pain and agony, of successes and failures. At least, mankind would no longer be drifting towards anarchy. Man would be deliberately shaping—reshaping—his society, turning topsyturvy an ancient and obsolete economy, good enough in its time but no longer applicable. At the same time, he would be tearing down the old cities and restoring Nature to something of its pristine condition, healing savage wounds inflicted by senseless selfish men in the past, cleansing the air, the poisoned rivers and lakes, growing new forests, permitting the wild creatures to flourish in their redeemed land. Man, the greedy savage child, had stripped the earth, killed the wild, fouled his own nest.

His anger, he suddenly realized, had been to divert him from that other feeling. Somehow, he had betrayed an ideal. He could not define the betrayal, because he knew that he was doing what had to be done and that that way was the only way. But he, and Kingbrook, Corrigan, and Beaucamp, had also felt this. He had seen it on their faces, like ectoplasm escaping the grasp of their minds.

A man had to be realistic. To gain one thing, you had to give up another. Life—the universe —was give and take, input and output, energy surrendered to conquer energy.

In short, politics. Compromises.

The door slid into the recess in the walls. Five men single-filed in. The President weighed each in the balance, anticipating his arguments and visualizing the bait which he would grab even if he saw the hook.

He said, "Gentlemen, be seated if you wish."

He looked at his watch and began to talk.

RIDERS OF THE PURPLE WAGE
or
The Great Gavage

If Jules Verne could really have looked into the future, say 1966 A.D., he would have crapped in his pants. And 2166, oh, my!

—from Grandpa Winnegan's unpublished Ms. *How I Screwed Uncle Sam & Other Private Ejaculations.*

THE COCK THAT CROWED BACKWARDS

Un and Sub, the giants, are grinding him for bread.

Broken pieces float up through the wine of sleep. Vast treadings crush abysmal grapes for the incubus sacrament.

He as Simple Simon fishes in his soul as
pail for the leviathan.

He groans, half-wakes, turns over, sweating
dark oceans, and groans again. Un and Sub,
putting their backs to their work, turn the
stone wheels of the sunken mill, muttering
Fie, fye, fo, fum. Eyes glittering orange-red as
a cat's in a cubbyhole, teeth dull white digits
in the murky arithmetic.

Un and Sub, Simple Simons themselves,
busily mix metaphors non-self-consciously.

Dunghill and cock's egg: up rises the cocka-
trice and gives first crow, two more to come,
in the flushrush of blood of dawn of I-am-the-
erection-and-the-strife.

It grows out and out until weight and length
merge to curve it over, a not-yet weeping
willow or broken reed. The one-eyed red head
peeks over the edge of bed. It rests its chinless
jaw, then, as body swells, slides over and
down. Looking monocularly this way and
those, it sniffs archaically across the floor
and heads for the door, left open by the lapsus
linguae of malingering sentinels.

A loud braying from the center of the room
makes it turn back. The three-legged ass,
Baalim's easel, is heehawing. On the easel is
the "canvas," an oval shallow pan of irradiated plastic, specially treated. The canvas is
two meters high and forty-four centimeters
deep. Within the painting is a scene that must
be finished by tomorrow.

As much sculpture as painting, the figures

are in alto-relief, rounded, some nearer the back of the pan than others. They glow with light from outside and also from the self-luminous plastic of the "canvas." The light seems to enter the figures, soak awhile, then break loose. The light is pale red, the red of dawn, of blood watered with tears, of anger, of ink on the debit side of the ledger.

This is one of his Dog Series: *Dogmas from a Dog, The Aerial Dogfight, Dog Days, the Sundog, Dog Reversed, The Dog of Flinders, Dog Berries, Dog Catcher, Lying Doggo, The Dog of the Right Angle* and *Improvisations on a Dog*.

Socrates, Ben Jonson, Cellini, Swedenborg, Li Po, and Hiawatha are roistering in the Mermaid Tavern. Through a window, Daedalus is seen on top of the battlements of Cnossus, shoving a rocket up the ass of his son, Icarus, to give him a jet-assisted takeoff for his famous flight. In one corner crouches Og, Son of Fire. He gnaws on a sabertooth bone and paints bison and mammoths on the mildewed plaster. The barmaid, Athena, is bending over the table where she is serving nectar and pretzels to her distinguished customers. Aristotle, wearing goat's horns, is behind her. He has lifted her skirt and is tupping her from behind. The ashes from the cigarette dangling from his smirking lips have fallen onto her skirt, which is beginning to smoke. In the doorway of the men's room, a drunken Batman succumbs to a long-pressed desire and attempts to bugger the Boy Wonder. Through

another window is a lake on the surface of
which a man is walking, a green-tarnished
halo hovering over his head. Behind him a
periscope sticks out of the water.

Prehensile, the penisnake wraps itself
around the brush and begins to paint. The
brush is a small cylinder attached at one end
to a hose which runs to a dome-shaped machine. From the other end of the cylinder extends a nozzle. The aperture of this can be
decreased or increased by rotation of a
thumb-dial on the cylinder. The paint which
the nozzle deposits in a fine spray or in a thick
stream or in whatever color or hue desired is
controlled by several dials on the cylinder.

Furiously, proboscisean, it builds up another figure layer by layer. Then, it sniffs a
musty odor of must and drops the brush and
slides out the door and down the bend of wall
of oval hall, describing the scrawl of legless
creatures, a writing in the sand which all may
read but few understand. Blood pumppumps
in rhythm with the mills of Un and Sub to feed
and swill the hot-blooded reptile. But the
walls, detecting intrusive mass and extrusive
desire, glow.

He groans, and the glandular cobra rises
and sways to the fluting of his wish for cunt-
cealment. Let there not be light! The lights
must be his cloaka. Speed past mother's
room, nearest the exit. Ah! Sighs softly in
relief but air whistles through the vertical
and tight mouth, announcing the departure of

the exsupress for Desideratum.

The door has become archaic; it has a keyhole. Quick! Up the ramp and out of the house through the keyhole and out onto the street. One person abroad a broad, a young woman with phosphorescent silver hair and snatch to match.

Out and down the street and coiling around her ankle. She looks down with surprise and then fear. He likes this; too willing were too many. He's found a diamond in the ruff.

Up around her kitten-ear-soft leg, around and around, and sliding across the dale of groin. Nuzzling the tender corkscrewed hairs and then, self-Tantalus, detouring up the slight convex of belly, saying hello to the bellybutton, pressing on it to ring upstairs, around and around the narrow waist and shyly and quickly snatching a kiss from each nipple. Then back down to form an expedition for climbing the mons veneris and planting the flag thereon.

Oh, delectation tabu and sickersacrosanct! There's a baby in there, ectoplasm beginning to form in eager preanticipation of actuality. Drop, egg, and shoot the chuty-chutes of flesh, hastening to gulp the lucky Micromoby Dick, outwriggling its million million brothers, survival of the fightingest.

A vast croaking fills the hall. The hot breath chills the skin. He sweats. Icicles coat the tumorous fuselage, and it sags under the weight of ice, and fog rolls around, whistling

past the struts, and the ailerons and elevators
are locked in ice, and he's losing altitude fast.
Get up, get up! Venusberg somewhere ahead
in the mists; Tannhäuser, blow your strum-
pets, send up your flares, I'm in a nose-
dive.

Mother's door has opened. A toad squatfills
the ovoid doorway. Its dewlap rises and falls
bellows-like; its toothless mouth gawps.
Ginungagap. Forked tongue shoots out and
curls around the boar cunstrictor. He cries
out with both mouths and jerks this way and
those. The waves of denial run through. Two
webbed paws bend and tie the flopping body
into a knot—a runny shapeshank, of course.

The woman strolls on. Wait for me! Out the
flood roars, crashes into the knot, roars back,
ebb clashing with flood. Too much and only
one way to go. He jerkspurts, the firmament
of waters falling, no Noah's ark or arc; he
novas, a shatter of millions of glowing wrig-
gling meteors, flashes in the pan of existence.

Thigh kingdom come. Groin and belly en-
cased in musty armor, and he cold, wet, and
trembling.

GOD'S PATENT ON DAWN EXPIRES

. . . the following spoken by Alfred Melophon
Voxpopper, of the Aurora Pushups and Coffee

Hour, Chanel 69B. Lines taped during the 50th Folk Art Center Annual Demonstration and Competition, Beverly Hills, level 14. Spoken by Omar Bacchylides Runic, extemporaneously if you discount some forethought during the previous evening at the nonpublic tavern, The Private Universe, and you may because Runic did not remember a thing about that evening. Despite which he won First Laurel Wreath A, there being no Second, Third, etc., wreaths classified as A through Z, God bless our democracy.

A gray-pink salmon leaping up the falls of
    night
Into the spawning pool of another day.

Dawn—the red roar of the heliac bull
Charging over the horizon.

The photonic blood of bleeding night,
Stabbed by the assassin sun.

and so on for fifty lines punctuated and fractured by cheers, handclaps, boos, hisses, and yelps.

Chib is half-awake. He peeps down into the narrowing dark as the dream roars off into the subway tunnel. He peeps through barely opened lids at the other reality: consciousness.

"Let my peeper go!" he groans with Moses

and so, thinking of long beards and horns
(courtesy of Michelangelo), he thinks of his
great-great-grandfather.

The will, a crowbar, forces his eyelids open.
He sees the fido which spans the wall opposite
him and curves up over half the ceiling. Dawn,
the paladin of the sun, is flinging its gray
gauntlet down.

Channel 69B, YOUR FAVORITE CHAN-
NEL, LA's own, brings you dawn. (Deception
in depth. Nature's false dawn shadowed forth
with electrons shaped by devices shaped by
man.)

Wake up with the sun in your heart and a
song on your lips! Thrill to the stirring lines
of Omar Runic! See dawn as the birds in the
trees, as God, see it!

Voxpopper chants the lines softly while
Grieg's *Anitra* wells softly. The old Norwe-
gian never dreamed of this audience and just
as well. A young man, Chibiabos Elgreco
Winnegan, has a sticky wick, courtesy of a
late gusher in the oilfield of the unconscious.

"Off your ass and onto your steed," Chib
says. "Pegasus runs today."

He speaks, thinks, lives in the present
tensely.

Chib climbs out of bed and shoves it into the
wall. To leave the bed sticking out, rumpled
as an old drunkard's tongue, would fracture
the aesthetics of his room, destroy that curve
that is the reflection of the basic universe, and
hinder him in his work.

The room is a huge ovoid and in a corner is a small ovoid, the toilet and shower. He comes out of it looking like one of Homer's god-like Achaeans, massively thighed, great-armed, golden-brown-skinned, blue-eyed, auburn-haired—although beardless. The phone is simulating the tocsin of a South American tree frog he once heard over Channel 122.

"Open O sesame!"

INTER CAECOS REGNAT LUSCUS

The face of Rex Luscus spreads across the fido, the pores of skin like the cratered fields of a World War I battlefield. He wears a black monocle over the left eye, ripped out in a brawl among art critics during the *I Love Rembrandt Lecture Series*, Channel 109. Although he has enough pull to get a priority for eye-replacement, he has refused.

"Inter caecos regnat luscus," he says when asked about it and quite often when not. "Translation: among the blind, the one-eyed man is king. That's why I renamed myself Rex Luscus, that is, King One-eyed."

There is a rumor, fostered by Luscus, that he will permit the bioboys to put in an artificial protein eye when he sees the works of an artist great enough to justify focal vision. It is also rumored that he may do so soon, because of his discovery of Chibiabos Elgreco Winnegan.

Luscus looks hungrily (he swears by adverbs) at Chib's tomentum and outlying regions. Chib swells, not with tumescence but with anger.

Luscus says, smoothly, "Honey, I just want to reassure myself that you're up and about the tremendously important business of this day. You must be ready for the showing, must! But now I see you, I'm reminded I've not eaten yet. What about breakfast with me?"

"What're we eating?" Chib says. He does not wait for a reply. "No. I've too much to do today. Close O sesame!"

Rex Luscus' face fades away, goatlike, or, as he prefers to describe it, the face of Pan, a Faunus of the arts. He has even had his ears trimmed to a point. Real cute.

"Baa-aa-aa!" Chib bleats at the phantom. "Ba! Humbuggery! I'll never kiss your ass, Luscus, or let you kiss mine. Even if I lose the grant!"

The phone bells again. The dark face of Rousseau Red Hawk appears. His nose is as the eagle's, and his eyes are broken black glass. His broad forehead is bound with a strip of red cloth, which circles the straight black hair that glides down to his shoulders. His shirt is buckskin; a necklace of beads hangs from his neck. He looks like a Plains Indian, although Sitting Bull, Crazy Horse, or the noblest Roman Nose of them all would have kicked him out of the tribe. Not that they were anti-Semitic, they just could not have respected a brave who broke out into hives when near a horse.

Born Julius Applebaum, he legally became Rousseau Red Hawk on his Naming Day. Just returned from the forest reprimevalized, he is now reveling in the accursed fleshpots of a decadent civilization.

"How're you, Chib? The gang's wondering how soon you'll get here?"

"Join you? I haven't had breakfast yet, and I've a thousand things to do to get ready for the showing. I'll see you at noon!"

"You missed out on the fun last night. Some goddam Egyptians tried to feel the girls up, but we salaamed them against the walls."

Rousseau vanished like the last of the red men.

Chib thinks of breakfast just as the intercom whistles. Open O sesame! He sees the living room. Smoke, too thick and furious for the air-conditioning to whisk away, roils. At the far end of the ovoid, his little half-brother and half-sister sleep on a flato. Playing Mama-and-friend, they fell asleep, their mouths open in blessed innocence, beautiful as only sleeping children can be. Opposite the closed eyes of each is an unwinking eye like that of a Mongolian Cyclops.

"Ain't's they cute?" Mama says. "The darlings were just too tired to toddle off."

The table is round. The aged knights and ladies are gathered around it for the latest quest of the ace, king, queen, and jack. They are armored only in layer upon layer of fat. Mama's jowls hang down like banners on a windless day. Her breasts creep and quiver on the table, bulge, and ripple.

"A gam of gamblers," he says aloud, looking at the fat faces, the tremendous tits, the rampant rumps. They raise their eyebrows. What the hell's the mad genius talking about now?

"Is your kid really retarded?" says one of Mama's friends, and they laugh and drink some more beer. Angela Ninon, not wanting to miss out on this deal and figuring Mama will soon turn on the sprayers anyway, pisses down her leg. They laugh at this, and William Conqueror says, "I open."

"I'm always open," Mama says, and they shriek with laughter.

Chib would like to cry. He does not cry, although he has been encouraged from childhood to cry any time he feels like it.

—It makes you feel better and look at the Vikings, what men they were and they cried like babies whenever they felt like it— Courtesy of Channel 202 on the popular program *What's A Mother Done?*

He does not cry because he feels like a man who thinks about the mother he loved and who is dead but who died a long time ago. His mother has been long buried under a landslide of flesh. When he was sixteen, he had had a lovely mother.

Then she cut him off.

THE FAMILY THAT BLOWS IS THE FAMILY THAT GROWS

> —from a poem by Edgar A. Grist, via Channel 88.

"Son, I don't get much out of this. I just do it because I love you."

Then, fat, fat, fat! Where did she go? Down into the adipose abyss. Disappearing as she grew larger.

"Sonny, you could at least wrestle with me a little now and then."

"You cut me off, Mama. That was all right. I'm a big boy now. But you haven't any right to expect me to want to take it up again."

"You don't love me any more!"

"What's for breakfast, Mama?" Chib says.

"I'm holding a good hand, Chibby," Mama says. "As you've told me so many times, you're a big boy. Just this once, get your own breakfast."

"What'd you call me for?"

"I forgot when your exhibition starts. I wanted to get some sleep before I went."

"14:30, Mama, but you don't have to go."

Rouged green lips part like a gangrened wound. She scratches one rouged nipple. "Oh, I want to be there. I don't want to miss my own son's artistic triumphs. Do you think you'll get the grant?"

"If I don't, it's Egypt for us," he says.

"Those stinking Arabs!" says William Conqueror.

"It's the Bureau that's doing it, not the Arabs," Chib says. "The Arabs moved for the same reason we may have to move."

From Grandpa's unpublished Ms.: Whoever would have thought that Beverly Hills would become anti-Semitic?

"I don't want to go to Egypt!" Mama wails. "You got to get that grant, Chibby. I don't want to leave the clutch. I was born and raised here, well, on the tenth level, anyway, and when I moved all my friends went along. I won't go!"

"Don't cry, Mama," Chib says, feeling distress despite himself. "Don't cry. The government can't force you to go, you know. You got your rights."

"If you want to keep on having goodies, you'll go," says Conqueror. "Unless Chib wins the grant, that is. And I wouldn't blame him if he didn't even try to win it. It ain't his fault you can't say no to Uncle Sam. You got your purple and the yap Chib makes from selling his paintings. Yet it ain't enough. You spend faster than you get it."

Mama screams with fury at William, and they're off. Chib cuts off fido. Hell with breakfast; he'll eat later. His final painting for the

Festival must be finished by noon. He presses a plate, and the bare egg-shaped room opens here and there, and painting equipment comes out like a gift from the electronic gods. Zeuxis would flip and Van Gogh would get the shakes if they could see the canvas and palette and brush Chib uses.

The process of painting involves the individual bending and twisting of thousands of wires into different shapes at various depths. The wires are so thin they can be seen only with magnifiers and manipulated with exceedingly delicate pliers. Hence, the goggles he wears and the long almost-gossamer instrument in his hand when he is in the first stages of creating a painting. After hundreds of hours of slow and patient labor (of love), the wires are arranged.

Chib removes his goggles to perceive the overall effect. He then uses the paint-sprayer to cover the wires with the colors and hues he desires. The paint dries hard within a few minutes. Chib attaches electrical leads to the pan and presses a button to deliver a tiny voltage through the wires. These glow beneath the paint and, Lilliputian fuses, disappear in blue smoke.

The result is a three-dimensional work composed of hard shells of paint on several levels below the exterior shell. The shells are of varying thicknesses and all are so thin that light slips through the upper to the inner shell when the painting is turned at angles. Parts of the shells are simply reflectors to intensify the light so that the inner images may be more visible.

When being shown, the painting is on a self-moving pedestal which turns the painting 12 degrees to the left from the center.

The fido tocsins. Chib, cursing, thinks of disconnecting it. At least, it's not the intercom with his mother calling hysterically. Not yet, anyway. She'll call soon enough if she loses heavily at poker.

Open O sesame!

SING, O MEWS, OF UNCLE SAM

Grandpa writes in his *Private Ejaculations:* Twenty-five years after I fled with twenty billion dollars and then supposedly died of a heart attack, Falco Accipiter is on my trail again. The IRB detective who named himself Falcon Hawk when he entered his profession. What an egotist! Yet, he is as sharp-eyed and relentless as a bird of prey, and I would shiver if I were not too old to be frightened by mere human beings. Who loosed the jesses and hood? How did he pick up the old and cold scent?

Accipiter's face is that of an overly suspicious peregrine that tries to look everywhere while it soars, that peers up its own anus to make sure that no duck has taken refuge there. The pale blue eyes fling glances like knives shot out of a shirtsleeve and hurled with a twist of the wrist. They scan all with sherlockian intake of minute and signifi-cant-detail. His head turns back and forth, ears twitching, nostrils expanding and col-lapsing, all radar and sonar and odar.

"Mr. Winnegan, I'm sorry to call so early. Did I get you out of bed?"

"It's obvious you didn't!" Chib says. "Don't bother to introduce yourself. I know you. You've been shadowing me for three days."

Accipiter does not redden. Master of control, he does all his blushing in the depths of his bowels, where no one can see. "If you know me, perhaps you can tell me why I'm calling you?"

"Would I be dumbshit enough to tell you?"

"Mr. Winnegan, I'd like to talk to you about your great-great-grandfather."

"He's been dead for twenty-five years!" Chib cries. "Forget him. And don't bother me. Don't try for a search warrant. No judge would give you one. A man's home is his hassle . . . I mean castle."

He thinks of Mama and what the day is going to be like unless he gets out soon. But he has to finish the painting.

"Fade off, Accipiter," Chib says. "I think I'll report you to the BPHR. I'm sure you got a fido inside that silly-looking hat of yours."

Accipiter's face is as smooth and unmoving as an alabaster carving of the falcon-god Horus. He may have a little gas bulging his intestines. If so, he slips it out unnoticed.

"Very well, Mr. Winnegan. But you're not getting rid of me that easily. After all . . ."

"Fade out!"

The intercom whistles thrice. What I tell you three times is Grandpa. "I was eavesdropping," says the 120-year-old voice, hollow and deep as an echo from a Pharaoh's tomb. "I want to see you before you leave. That is, if you can spare the Ancient of Daze a few minutes."

"Always, Grandpa," Chib says, thinking of how much he loves the old man. "You need any food?"

"Yes, and for the mind, too."

Der Tag. Dies Irae. Götterdämmerung. Armageddon. Things are closing in. Make-or-break day. Go-no-go time. All these calls and a feeling of more to come. What will the end of the day bring?

THE TROCHE SUN SLIPS INTO THE SORE THROAT OF NIGHT
—from Omar Runic

Chib walks towards the convex door, which rolls into the interstices between the walls.

The focus of the house is the oval family room. In the first quadrant, going clockwise, is the kitchen, separated from the family room by six-meter-high accordion screens, painted with scenes from Egyptian tombs by Chib, his too subtle comment on modern food. Seven slim pillars around the family room mark the borders of room and corridor. Between the pillars are more tall accordion screens, painted by Chib during his Amerind mythology phase.

The corridor is also oval-shaped; every room in the house opens onto it. There are seven rooms, six bedroom-workroom-study-toilet-shower combinations. The seventh is a storeroom.

Little eggs within bigger eggs within great eggs within a megamonolith on a planetary pear within an ovoid universe, the latest cosmogony indicating that infinity has the form of a hen's fruit. God broods over the abyss and cackles every trillion years or so.

Chib cuts across the hall, passes between two pillars, carved by him into nymphet caryatids, and enters the family room. His mother looks sidewise at her son, who she thinks is rapidly approaching insanity if he has not already overshot his mark. It's partly her fault; she shouldn't have gotten disgusted and in a moment of wackiness called It off. Now, she's fat and ugly, oh, God, so fat and ugly. She can't reasonably or even unreasonably hope to start up again.

It's only natural, she keeps telling herself, sighing, resentful, teary, that he's abandoned the love of his mother for the strange, firm, shapely delights of young women. But to give them up, too? He's not a bisex. He quit all that when he was thirteen. So what's the reason for his chastity? He isn't in love with the fornixator, either, which she would understand, even if she did not approve.

Oh, God, where did I go wrong? And then, There's nothing wrong with me. He's going crazy like his father—Raleigh Renaissance, I think his name was—and his aunt and his great-great-grandfather. It's all that painting and those radicals, the Young Radishes, he runs around with. He's too artistic, too sensitive. Oh, God, if something happens to my little boy, I'll have to go to Egypt.

Chib knows her thoughts since she's voiced them so many times and is not capable of having new ones. He passes the round table without a word. The knights and ladies of the canned Camelot see him through a beery veil.

In the kitchen, he opens an oval door in the wall. He removes a tray with food in covered dishes and cups, all wrapped in plastic.

"Aren't you going to eat with us?"

"Don't whine, Mama," he says and goes back to his room to pick up some cigars for his Grandpa. The door, detecting, amplifying, and transmitting the shifting but recognizable eidolon of epidermal electrical fields to the activating mechanism, balks. Chib is too upset. Magnetic maelstroms rage over his skin and distort the spectral configuration. The door half-rolls out, rolls in, changes its minds again, rolls out, rolls in.

Chib kicks the door and it becomes completely blocked. He decides he'll have a video or vocal sesame put in. Trouble is, he's short of units and coupons and can't buy the materials. He shrugs and walks along the curving, one-walled hall and stops in front of Grandpa's door, hidden from view of those in the living room by the kitchen screens.

"For he sang of peace and freedom,
Sang of beauty, love, and longing;
Sang of death, and life undying
In the Islands of the Blessed,
In the kingdom of Ponemah,
In the land of the Hereafter.
Very dear to Hiawatha
Was the gentle Chibiabos."

Chib chants the passwords; the door rolls back.

Light glares out, a yellowish red-tinged light that is Grandpa's own creation. Looking into the convex oval door is like looking into the lens of a madman's eyeball. Grandpa, in the middle of the room, has a white beard falling to midthigh and white hair cataracting to just below the back of his knees. Although beard and headhair conceal his nakedness, and he is not out in public, he wears a pair of shorts. Grandpa is somewhat old-fashioned, forgivable in a man of twelve decadencies.

Like Rex Luscus, he is one-eyed. He smiles with his own teeth, grown from buds transplanted thirty years ago. A big green cigar sticks out of one corner of his full red mouth. His nose is broad and smeared as if time had stepped upon it with a heavy foot. His forehead and cheeks are broad, perhaps due to a shot of Ojibway blood in his veins, though he was born Finnegan and even sweats celtically, giving off an aroma of whiskey. He holds his head high, and the blue-gray eye is like a pool at the bottom of a prediluvian pothole, remnant of a melted glacier.

All in all, Grandpa's face is Odin's as he returns from the Well of Mimir, wondering if he paid too great a price. Or it is the face of the windbeaten, sandblown Sphinx of Gizeh.

"Forty centuries of hysteria look down upon you, to paraphrase Napoleon," Grandpa says. "The rockhead of the ages. *What, then is Man?* sayeth the New Sphinx, Oedipus having resolved the question of the Old Sphinx and settling nothing because She had already delivered another of her kind, a smartass kid with a question nobody's been able to answer yet. And perhaps just as well it can't be."

"You talk funny," Chib says. "But I like it."

He grins at Grandpa, loving him.

"You sneak into here every day, not so much from love for me as to gain knowledge and insight. I have seen all, heard everything, and thought more than a little. I voyaged much before I took refuge in this room a quarter of a century ago. Yet confinement here has been the greatest Odyssey of all.

THE ANCIENT MARINATOR

I call myself. A marinade of wisdom steeped in the brine of over-salted cynicism and too long a life."

"You smile so, you must have just had a woman," Chib teases.

"No, my boy. I lost the tension in my ram-rod thirty years ago. And I thank God for that, since it removes from me the temptation of fornication, not to mention masturbation. However, I have other energies left, hence, scope for other sins, and these are even more serious.

"Aside from the sin of sexual commission, which paradoxically involves the sin of sexual emission, I had other reasons for not asking that Old Black Magician Science for shots to starch me out again. I was too old for young girls to be attracted to me for anything but money. And I was too much a poet, a lover of beauty, to take on the wrinkled blisters of my generation or several just before mine.

"So now you see, my son. My clapper swings limberly in the bell of my sex. Ding, dong, ding, dong. A lot of dong, but not much ding."

Grandpa laughs deeply, a lion's roar with a spray of doves.

"I am but the mouthpiece of the ancients, a shyster pleading for long-dead clients. Come not to bury but to praise and forced by my sense of fairness to admit the faults of the past, too. I'm a queer crabbed old man, pent like Merlin in his tree trunk. Samolxis, the Thracian bear god, hibernating in his cave. The Last of the Seven Sleepers."

Grandpa goes to the slender plastic tube depending from the ceiling and pulls down the folding handles of the eyepiece.

"Accipiter is hovering outside our house. He smells something rotten in Beverly Hills, level 14. Could it be that Win-again Winnegan isn't dead? Uncle Sam is like a diplodocus kicked in the ass. It takes twenty-five years for the message to reach its brain."

Tears appear in Chib's eyes. He says, "Oh, God, Grandpa, I don't want anything to happen to you."

"What can happen to a 120-year-old man besides failure of brain or kidneys?"

"With all due respect, Grandpa," Chib says, "you do rattle on."

"Call me Id's mill," Grandpa says. "The flour it yields is baked in the strange oven of my ego—or half-baked, if you please."

Chib grins through his tears and says, "They taught me at school that puns are cheap and vulgar."

"What's good enough for Homer, Aristophanes, Rabelais, and Shakespeare is good enough for me. By the way, speaking of cheap and vulgar, I met your mother in the hall last night, before the poker party started. I was just leaving the kitchen with a bottle of booze. She almost fainted. But she recovered fast and pretended not to see me. Maybe she did think she'd seen a ghost. I doubt it. She'd have been blabbing all over town about it."

"She may have told her doctor," Chib says. "She saw you several weeks ago, remember? She may have mentioned it while she was bitching about her so-called dizzy spells and hallucinations."

"And the old sawbones, knowing the family history, called the IRB. Maybe."

Chib looks through the periscope's eyepiece. He rotates it and turns the knobs on the handle-ends to raise and lower the cyclops on the end of the tube outside. Accipiter is stalking around the aggregate of seven eggs, each on the end of a broad thin curved branchlike walk projecting from the central pedestal. Accipiter goes up the steps of a branch to the door of Mrs. Applebaum's. The door opens.

"He must have caught her away from the fornixator," Chib says. "And she must be lonely; she's not talking to him over fido. My God, she's fatter than Mama!"

"Why not?" Grandpa says. "Mr. and Mrs. Everyman sit on their asses all day, drink, eat,

and watch fido, and their brains run to mud
and their bodies to sludge. Caesar would have
had no trouble surrounding himself with fat
friends these days. You ate, too, Brutus?"

Grandpa's comment, however, should not
apply to Mrs. Applebaum. She has a hole in
her head, and people addicted to fornixation
seldom get fat. They sit or lie all day and part
of the night, the needle in the fornix area
of the brain delivering a series of minute
electrical jolts. Indescribable ecstasy floods
through their bodies with every impulse, a delight far surpassing any of food, drink, or sex.
It's illegal, but the government never bothers
a user unless it wants to get him for something else, since a fornic rarely has children.
Twenty per cent of LA have had holes drilled
in their heads and tiny shafts inserted for
access of the needle. Five per cent are addicted; they waste away, seldom eating,
their distended bladders spilling poisons into
the bloodstream.

Chib says, "My brother and sister must
have seen you sometimes when you were
sneaking out to mass. Could they . . . ?"

"They think I'm a ghost, too. In this day and
age! Still, maybe it's a good sign that they can
believe in something, even a spook."

"You better stop sneaking out to Church."

"The Church, and you, are the only things
that keep me going. It was a sad day, though,
when you told me you couldn't believe. You
would have made a good priest—with faults,

of course—and I could have had private mass and confession in this room."

Chib says nothing. He's gone to instruction and observed services just to please Grandpa. The Church was an egg-shaped seashell which, held to the ear, gave only the distant roar of God receding like an ebb tide.

THERE ARE UNIVERSES BEGGING FOR GODS

yet He hangs around this one looking for work.

—from Grandpa's Ms.

Grandpa takes over the eyepiece. He laughs. "The Internal Revenue Bureau! I thought it'd been disbanded! Who the hell has an income big enough to report on any more? Do you suppose it's still active just because of me? Could be."

He calls Chib back to the scope, directed towards the center of Beverly Hills. Chib has a lane of vision between the seven-egged clutches on the branched pedestals. He can see part of the central plaza, the giant ovoids of the city hall, the federal bureaus, the Folk Center, part of the massive spiral on which set the houses of worship, and the dora (from pandora) where those on the purple wage get their goods and those with extra income get their goodies. One end of the big artificial lake is visible; boats and canoes sail on it and people fish.

The irradiated plastic dome that enfolds the clutches of Beverly Hills is sky-blue. The electronic sun climbs towards the zenith. There are a few white genuine-looking images of clouds and even a V of geese migrating south, their honks coming down faintly. Very nice for those who have never been outside the walls of LA. But Chib spent two years in the World Nature Rehabilitation and Conservation Corps—the WNRCC—and he knows the difference. Almost, he decided to desert with Rousseau Red Hawk and join the neo-Amerinds. Then, he was going to become a forest ranger. But this might mean he'd end up shooting or arresting Red Hawk. Besides, he didn't want to become a sammer. And he wanted more than anything to paint.

"There's Rex Luscus," Chib says. "He's being interviewed outside the Folk Center. Quite a crowd."

THE PELLUCIDAR BREAKTHROUGH

Luscus' middle name should have been Upmanship. A man of great erudition, with privileged access to the Library of Greater LA computer, and of Ulyssean sneakiness, he is always scoring over his colleagues.

He it was who founded the Go-Go School of Criticism.

Primalux Ruskinson, his great competitor, did some extensive research when Luscus announced the title of his new philosophy. Ruskinson triumphantly announced that Luscus had taken the phrase from obsolete slang, current in the mid-twentieth century.

Luscus, in the fido interview next day, said that Ruskinson was a rather shallow scholar, which was to be expected.

Go-go was taken from the Hottentot language. In Hottentot, *go-go* meant to examine, that is, to keep looking until something about the object—in this case, the artist and his works—has been observed.

The critics got in line to sign up at the new school. Ruskinson thought of committing suicide, but instead accused Lascus of having blown his way up the ladder of success.

Lascus replied on fido that his personal life was his own, and Ruskinson was in danger of being sued for violation of privacy. However, he deserved no more effort than a man striking at a mosquito.

"What the hell's a mosquito?" say millions of viewers. "Wish the bighead would talk language we could understand."

Luscus' voice fades off for a minute while the interpreters explain, having just been slipped a note from a monitor who's run off the word through the station's encyclopedia.

Luscus rode on the novelty of the Go-Go School for two years.

Then he re-established his prestige, which had been slipping somewhat, with his philosophy of the Totipotent Man.

This was so popular that the Bureau of Cultural Development and Recreation requisitioned a daily one-hour slot for a year-and-a-half in the initial program of totipotentializing.

Grandpa Winnegan's penned comment in his *Private Ejaculations:*

What about The Totipotent Man, that apotheosis of individuality and complete psychosomatic development, the democratic Ubermensch, as recommended by Rex Luscus, the sexually one-sided? Poor old Uncle Sam! Trying to force the proteus of his citizens into a single stabilized shape so he can control them. And at the same time trying to encourage each and every to bring to flower his inherent capabilities—if any! The poor old long-legged, chin-whiskered, milk-hearted, flint-brained schizophrenic! Verily, the left hand knows not what the right hand is doing. As a matter of fact, the right hand doesn't know what the right hand is doing.

"What about the totipotent man?" Luscus

replied to the chairman during the fourth session of the *Luscan Lecture Series.* "How does he conflict with the contemporary Zeitgeist? He doesn't. The totipotent man is the imperative of our times. He must come into being before the Golden World can be realized. How can you have a Utopia without utopians, a Golden World with humans of brass?"

It was during this Memorable Day that Luscus gave his talk on The Pellucidar Breakthrough and thereby made Chibiabos Winnegan famous. And more than incidentally gave Luscus his biggest score over his competitors.

"Pellucidar? Pellucidar?" Ruskinson mutters. "Oh, God, what's Tinker Bell doing now?"

"It'll take me some time to explain why I use this phrase to describe Winnegan's stroke of genius," Luscus continues. "First, let me seem to detour.

FROM THE ARCTIC TO ILLINOIS

"Now, Confucius once said that a bear could not fart at the North Pole without causing a big wind in Chicago.

"By this he meant that all events, therefore, all men, are interconnected in an unbreakable web. What one man does, no matter how seemingly insignificant, vibrates through the strands and affects every man."

Ho Chung Ko, before his fido on the 30th level of Lhasa, Tibet, says to his wife, "That white prick has got it all wrong. Confucius didn't say that. Lenin preserve us! I'm going to call him up and give him hell."

His wife says, "Let's change the channel. Pai Ting Place is on now, and . . ."

Ngombe, 10th level, Nairobi: "The critics here are a bunch of black bastards. Now you take Luscus; he could see my genius in a second. I'm going to apply for emigration in the morning."

Wife: "You might at least ask me if I want to go! What about the kids . . . mother . . . friends . . . dog . . . ?" and so on into the lionless night of self-luminous Africa.

" . . . ex-president Radinoff," Luscus continues, "once said that this is the 'Age of the Plugged-In Man.' Some rather vulgar remarks have been made about this, to me, insighted phrase. But Radinoff did not mean that human society is a daisy chain. He meant that the current of modern society flows through the circuit of which we are all part. This is the Age of Complete Interconnection. No wires can hang loose; otherwise we all short-circuit. Yet, it is undeniable that life without individuality is not worth living. Every man must be a *hapax legomenon...*"

Ruskinson jumps up from his chair and screams, "I know that phrase! I got you this time, Luscus!"

He is so excited he falls over in a faint, symptom of a widespread hereditary defect. When he recovers, the lecture is over. He springs to the recorder to run off what he missed. But Luscus has carefully avoided defining The Pellucidar Breakthrough. He will explain it at another lecture.

Grandpa, back at the scope, whistles. "I feel like an astronomer. The planets are in orbit around our house, the sun. There's Accipiter, the closest, Mercury, although he's not the god of thieves but their nemesis. Next, Benedictine, your sad-sack Venus. Hard, hard, hard! The sperm would batter their heads flat against the stony ovum. You sure she's pregnant?

"Your Mama's out there, dressed fit to kill and I wish someone would. Mother Earth headed for the perigee of the gummint store to waste your substance."

Grandpa braces himself as if on a rolling deck, the blue-black veins on his legs thick as strangling vines on an ancient oak. "Brief departure from the role of Herr Doktor Sternscheissdreckschnuppe, the great astronomer, to that of der Unterseeboot Kapitan von Schooten die Fischen in der Barrel. Ach! I zee yet das tramp schteamer, Deine Mama, yaw-

ing, pitching, rolling in the seas of alcohol.
Compass lost; rhumb dumb. Three sheets to
the wind. Paddlewheels spinning in the air.
The black gang sweating their balls off, stok-
ing the furnaces of frustration. Propeller
tangled in the nets of neurosis. And the Great
White Whale a glimmer in the black depths
but coming up fast, intent on broaching her
bottom, too big to miss. Poor damned vessel, I
weep for her. I also vomit with disgust.

"Fire one! Fire two! Baroom! Mama rolls
over, a jagged hole in her hull but not the one
you're thinking of. Down she goes, nose first,
as befits a devoted fellationeer, her huge aft
rising into the air. Blub, blub! Full fathom
five!

"And so back from undersea to outer space.
Your sylvan Mars, Red Hawk, has just
stepped out of the tavern. And Luscus,
Jupiter, the one-eyed All-Father of Art, if
you'll pardon my mixing of Nordic and Latin
mythologies, is surrounded by his swarm of
satellites."

EXCRETION IS THE BITTER PART
OF VALOR

Luscus says to the fido interviewers. "By this
I mean that Winnegan, like every artist, great
or not, produces art that is, first, secretion,

unique to himself, then excretion. Excretion in the original sense of 'sifting out.' Creative excretion or discrete excretion. I know that my distinguished colleagues will make fun of this analogy, so I hereby challenge them to a fido debate whenever it can be arranged.

"The valor comes from the courage of the artist in showing his inner products to the public. The bitter part comes from the fact that the artist may be rejected or misunderstood in his time. Also from the terrible war that takes place in the artist with the disconnected or chaotic elements, often contradictory, which he must unite and then mold into a unique entity. Hence my 'discrete excretion' phrase."

Fido interviewer: "Are we to understand that everything is a big pile of shit but that art makes a strange seachange, forms it into something golden and illuminating?"

"Not exactly. But you're close. I'll elaborate and expound at a later date. At present, I want to talk about Winnegan. Now, the lesser artists give only the surface of things; they are photographers. But the great ones give the interiority of objects and beings. Winnegan, however, is the first to reveal more than one interiority in a single work of art. His invention of the alto-relief multilevel technique enables him to epiphanize—show forth—subterranean layer upon layer."

Primalux Ruskinson, loudly, "The Great Onion Peeler of Painting!"

Luscus, calmly after the laughter has died: "In one sense, that is well put. Great art, like an onion, brings tears to the eyes. However, the light on Winnegan's paintings is not just a reflection; it is sucked in, digested, and then fractured forth. Each of the broken beams makes visible, not various aspects of the figures beneath, but whole figures. Worlds, I might say.

"I call this The Pellucidar Breakthrough. Pellucidar is the hollow interior of our planet, as depicted in a now forgotten fantasy-romance of the twentieth-century writer, Edgar Rice Burroughs, creator of the immortal Tarzan."

Ruskinson moans and feels faint again. "Pellucid! Pellucidar! Luscus, you punning exhumist bastard!"

"Burroughs' hero penetrated the crust of Earth to discover another world inside. This was, in some ways, the reverse of the exterior, continents where the surface seas are, and vice versa. Just so, Winnegan has discovered an inner world, the obverse of the public image Everyman projects. And, like Burroughs' hero, he has returned with a stunning narrative of psychic dangers and exploration.

"And just as the fictional hero found his Pellucidar to be populated with stone-age men and dinosaurs, so Winnegan's world is, though absolutely modern in one sense, archaic in another. Abysmally pristine. Yet, in the illumination of Winnegan's world, there is

an evil and inscrutable patch of blackness,
and that is paralleled in Pellucidar by the tiny
fixed moon which casts a chilling and unmoving shadow.

"Now, I did intend that the ordinary 'pellucid' should be part of Pellucidar. Yet
'pellucid' means 'reflecting light evenly from
all surfaces' or 'admitting maximum passage
of light without diffusion or distortion.' Winnegan's paintings do just the opposite. But—
under the broken and twisted light, the acute
observer can see a primeval luminosity, even
and straight. This is the light that links all the
fractures and multilevels, the light I was
thinking of in my earlier discussion of the
'Age of the Plugged-In Man' and the polar
bear.

"By intent scrutiny, a viewer may detect
this, feel, as it were, the photonic fremitus of
the heartbeat of Winnegan's world."

Ruskinson almost faints. Luscus' smile and
black monocle make him look like a pirate
who has just taken a Spanish galleon loaded
with gold.

Grandpa, still at the scope, says, "And
there's Maryam bint Yusuf, the Egyptian
backwoodswoman you were telling me about.
Your Saturn, aloof, regal, cold, and wearing
one of those suspended whirling manycolored
hats that're all the rage. Saturn's rings? Or a
halo?"

"She's beautiful, and she'd make a wonderful mother for my children," Chib says.

"The shock of Araby. Your Saturn has two
moons, mother and aunt. Chaperones! You
say she'd make a good mother! How good a
wife! Is she intelligent?"

"She's as smart as Benedictine."

"A dumbshit then. You sure can pick them.
How do you know you're in love with her?
You've been in love with twenty women in the
last six months."

"I love her. This is it."

"Until the next one. Can you really love anything but your painting? Benedictine's going
to have an abortion, right?"

"Not if I can talk her out of it," Chib says.
"To tell the truth, I don't even like her any
more. But she's carrying my child."

"Let me look at your pelvis. No, you're
male. For a moment, I wasn't sure, you're so
crazy to have a baby."

"A baby is a miracle to stagger sextillions of
infidels."

"It beats a mouse. But don't you know that
Uncle Sam has been propagandizing his heart
out to cut down on propagation? Where've
you been all your life?"

"I got to go, Grandpa."

Chib kisses the old man and returns to his
room to finish his latest painting. The door
still refuses to recognize him, and he calls the
gummint repair shop, only to be told that all
technicians are at the Folk Festival. He leaves
the house in a red rage. The bunting and bal-

loons are waving and bobbing in the artificial wind, increased for this occasion, and an orchestra is playing by the lake.

Through the scope, Grandpa watches him walk away.

"Poor devil! I ache for his ache. He wants a baby, and he is ripped up inside because that poor devil Benedictine is aborting their child. Part of his agony, though he doesn't know it, is identification with the doomed infant. His own mother has had innumerable—well, quite a few—abortions. But for the grace of God, he would have been one of them, another nothingness. He wants this baby to have a chance, too. But there is nothing he can do about it, nothing.

"And there is another feeling, one which he shares with most of humankind. He knows he's screwed up his life, or something has twisted it. Every thinking man and woman knows this. Even the smug and dimwitted realize this unconsciously. But a baby, that beautiful being, that unsmirched blank tablet, unformed angel, represents a new hope. Perhaps it won't screw up. Perhaps it'll grow up to be a healthy confident reasonable good-humored unselfish loving man or woman. 'It won't be like me or my next-door neighbor,' the proud, but apprehensive, parent swears.

"Chib thinks this and swears that his baby will be different. But, like everybody else, he's fooling himself. A child has one father and mother, but it has trillions of aunts and

uncles. Not only those that are its contemporaries; the dead, too. Even if Chib fled into the
wilderness and raised the infant himself, he'd
be giving it his own unconscious assumptions.
The baby would grow up with beliefs and attitudes that the father was not even aware of.
Moreover, being raised in isolation, the baby
would be a very peculiar human being indeed.

"And if Chib raises the child in this society,
it's inevitable that it will accept at least part
of the attitudes of its playmates, teachers, and
so on ad nauseam.

"So, forget about making a new Adam out
of your wonderful potential-teeming child,
Chib. If it grows up to become at least half-
sane, it's because you gave it love and discipline and it was lucky in its social contacts
and it was also blessed at birth with the right
combination of genes. That is, your son or
daughter is now both a fighter and a lover.

ONE MAN'S NIGHTMARE IS ANOTHER MAN'S WET DREAM

Grandpa says.

"I was talking to Dante Alighieri just the
other day, and he was telling me what an
inferno of stupidity, cruelty, perversity,

atheism, and outright peril the sixteenth century was. The nineteenth left him gibbering, hopelessly searching for adequate enough invectives.

"As for this age, it gave him such high-blood pressure, I had to slip him a tranquilizer and ship him out via time machine with an attendant nurse. She looked much like Beatrice and so should have been just the medicine he needed—maybe."

Grandpa chuckles, remembering that Chib, as a child, took him seriously, when he described his time-machine visitors, such notables as Nebuchadnezzar, King of the Grass-Eaters; Samson, Bronze Age Riddler and Scourge of the Philistines; Moses, who stole a god from his Kenite father-in-law and who fought against circumcision all his life; Buddha, the Original Beatnik; No-Moss Sisyphus, taking a vacation from his stone-rolling; Androcles and his buddy, the Cowardly Lion of Oz; Baron von Richthofen, the Red Knight of Germany; Beowulf; Al Capone; Hiawatha; Ivan the Terrible; and hundreds of others.

The time came when Grandpa became alarmed and decided that Chib was confusing fantasy with reality. He hated to tell the little boy that he had been making up all those wonderful stories, mostly to teach him history. It was like telling a kid there wasn't any Santa Claus.

And then, while he was reluctantly breaking the news to his grandson he became aware of

Chib's barely suppressed grin and knew that
it was his turn to have his leg pulled. Chib had
never been fooled or else had caught on
without any shock. So, both had a big laugh
and Grandpa continued to tell of his visitors.

"There are no time machines," Grandpa
says. "Like it or not, Miniver Cheevy, you have
to live in this your time.

"The machines work in the utility-factory
levels in a silence broken only by the chatter
of a few mahouts. The great pipes at the
bottom of the seas suck up water and bottom
sludge. The stuff is automatically carried
through pipes to the ten production levels of
LA. There the inorganic chemicals are converted into energy and then into the matter of
food, drink, medicines, and artifacts. There is
very little agriculture or animal husbandry
outside the city walls, but there is super-
abundance for all. Artificial but exact dupli-
cation of organic stuff, so who knows the
difference?

"There is no more starvation or want anywhere, except among the self-exiles wander-
ing in the woods. And the food and goods are
shipped to the pandoras and dispensed to
the receivers of the purple wage. *The purple
wage*. A Madison-Avenue euphemism with
connotations of royalty and divine right.
Earned by just being born.

"Other ages would regard ours as a
delirium, yet ours has benefits others lacked.
To combat transiency and rootlessness, the

megalopolis is compartmented into small communities. A man can live all his life in one place without having to go elsewhere to get anything he needs. With this has come a provincialism, a small-town patriotism and hostility towards outsiders. Hence, the bloody juvenile gang-fights between towns. The intense and vicious gossip. The insistence on conformity to local mores.

"At the same time, the small-town citizen has fido, which enables him to see events anywhere in the world. Intermingled with the trash and the propaganda, which the government thinks is good for the people, is any amount of superb programs. A man may get the equivalent of a Ph.D. without stirring out of his house.

"Another Renaissance has come, a fruition of the arts comparable to that of Pericles' Athens and the city-states of Michelangelo's Italy or Shakespeare's England. Paradox. More illiterates than ever before in the world's history. But also more literates. Speakers of classical Latin outnumber those of Caesar's day. The world of aesthetics bears a fabulous fruit. And, of course, fruits.

"To dilute the provincialism and also to make international war even more unlikely, we have the world policy of *homogenization*. The voluntary exchange of a part of one nation's population with another's. Hostages to peace and brotherly love. Those citizens who can't get along on just the purple wage or who think they'll be happier elsewhere are inducted to emigrate with bribes.

"A Golden World in some respects; a nightmare in others. So what's new with the world? It was always thus in every age. Ours has had to deal with overpopulation and automation. How else could the problem be solved? It's Buridan's ass (actually, the ass was a dog) all over again, as in every time. Buridan's ass, dying of hunger because it can't make up its mind which of two equal amounts of food to eat.

"History: *a pons asinorum* with men the asses on the bridge of time.

"No, those two comparisons are not fair or right. It's Hobson's horse, the only choice being the beast in the nearest stall. Zeitgeist rides tonight, and the devil take the hindmost!

"The mid-twentieth-century writers of the Triple Revolution document forecast accurately in some respects. But they deemphasized what lack of work would do to Mr. Everyman. They believed that all men have equal potentialities in developing artistic tendencies, that all could busy themselves with arts, crafts, and hobbies or education for education's sake. They wouldn't face the 'undemocratic' reality that only about ten per cent of the population—if that —are inherently capable of producing anything worth while, or even mildly interesting, in the arts. Crafts, hobbies, and a lifelong academic education pale after a while, so back to the booze, fido, and adultery.

"Lacking self-respect, the fathers become free-floaters, nomads on the steppes of sex. Mother, with a capital M, becomes the dominant figure in the family. She may be playing around, too, but she's taking care of the kids; she's around most of the time. Thus, with father a lower-case figure, absent, weak, or indifferent, the children often become homosexual or ambisexual. The wonderland is also a fairyland.

"Some features of this time could have been predicted. Sexual permissiveness was one, although no one could have seen how far it would go. But then no one could have foreknown of the Panamorite sect, even if America has spawned lunatic-fringe cults as a frog spawns tadpoles. Yesterday's monomaniac is tomorrow's messiah, and so Sheltey and his disciples survived through years of persecution and today their precepts are embedded in our culture."

Grandpa again fixes the cross-reticules of the scope on Chib.

"There he goes, my beautiful grandson, bearing gifts to the Greeks. So far, that Hercules has failed to clean up his psychic Augean stable. Yet, he may succeed, that stumblebum Apollo, that Edipus Wrecked. He's luckier than most of his contemporaries. He's had a permanent father, even if a secret one, a zany old man hiding from so-called justice. He has gotten love, discipline, and a

superb education in this starred chamber.
He's also fortunate in having a profession.

"But Mama spends far too much and also is
addicted to gambling, a vice which deprives
her of her full guaranteed income. I'm supposed to be dead, so I don't get the purple
wage. Chib has to make up for all this by
selling or trading his paintings. Luscus has
helped him by publicizing him, but at any
moment Luscus may turn against him. The
money from the paintings is still not enough.
After all, money is not the basic of our
economy; it's a scarce auxiliary. Chib needs
the grant but won't get it unless he lets Luscus
make love to him.

"It's not that Chib rejects homosexual re-
lations. Like most of his contemporaries, he's
sexually ambivalent. I think that he and Omar
Runic still blow each other occasionally. And
why not? They love each other. But Chib rejects Luscus as a matter of principle. He
won't be a whore to advance his career. Moreover, Chib makes a distinction which is deeply
embedded in this society. He thinks that un-
compulsive homosexuality is natural (whatever that means?) but that compulsive homosexuality is, to use an old term, queer. Valid
or not, the distinction is made.

"So, Chib may go to Egypt. But what happens to me then?

"Never mind me or your mother, Chib. No
matter what. Don't give in to Luscus. Remember the dying words of Singleton, Bureau of

Relocation and Rehabilitation Director, who shot himself because he couldn't adjust to the new times.

" 'What if a man gain the world and lose his ass?' "

At this moment, Grandpa sees his grandson, who has been walking along with somewhat drooping shoulders, suddenly straighten them. And he sees Chib break into a dance, a little improvised shuffle followed by a series of whirls. It is evident that Chib is whooping. The pedestrians around him are grinning.

Grandpa groans and then laughs. "Oh, God, the goatish energy of youth, the unpredictable shift of spectrum from black sorrow to bright orange joy! Dance, Chib, dance your crazy head off! Be happy, if only for a moment! You're young yet, you've got the bubbling of unconquerable hope deep in your springs! Dance, Chib, dance!"

He laughs and wipes a tear away.

SEXUAL IMPLICATIONS OF THE CHARGE OF THE LIGHT BRIGADE

is so fascinating a book that Doctor Jespersen Joyce Bathymens, psycholinguist for the federal Bureau of Group Reconfiguration and Intercommunicability, hates to stop reading. But duty beckons.

"A radish is not necessarily reddish," he says into the recorder. "The Young Radishes so named their group because a radish is a radicle, hence, radical. Also, there's a play on roots and on red-ass, a slang term for anger, and possibly on ruttish and rattish. And undoubtedly on rude-ickle, Beverly Hills dialectical term for a repulsive, unruly, and socially ungraceful person.

"Yet the Young Radishes are not what I would call Left Wing; they represent the current resentment against Life-In-General and advocate no radical policy of reconstruction. They howl against Things As They Are, like monkeys in a tree, but never give constructive criticism. They want to destroy without any thought of what to do after the destruction.

"In short, they represent the average citizen's grousing and bitching, being different in that they are more articulate. There are thousands of groups like them in LA and possibly millions all over the world. They had normal life as children. In fact, they were born and raised in the same clutch, which is one reason why they were chosen for this study. What phenomenon produced ten such creative persons, all mothered in the seven houses of Area 69-14, all about the same time, all practically raised together, since they were put together in the playpen on top of the pedestal while one mother took her turn baby-sitting and the others did whatever they had to do, which . . . where was I?

"Oh, yes, they had a normal life, went to the same school, palled around, enjoyed the usual sexual play among themselves, joined the juvenile gangs and engaged in some rather bloody warfare with the Westwood and other gangs. All were distinguished however, by an intense intellectual curiosity and all became active in the creative arts.

"It has been suggested—and might be true —that the mysterious stranger, Raleigh Renaissance, was the father of all ten. This is possible but can't be proved. Raleigh Renaissance was living in the house of Mrs. Winnegan at the time, but he seems to have been unusually active in the clutch, and, indeed, all over Beverly Hills. Where this man came from, who he was, and where he went are still unknown despite intensive search by various agencies. He had no ID or other cards of any kind yet he went unchallenged for a long time. He seems to have had something on the Chief of Police of Beverly Hills and possibly on some of the federal agents stationed in Beverly Hills.

"He lived for two years with Mrs. Winnegan, then dropped out of sight. It is rumored that he left LA to join a tribe of white neo-Amerinds, sometimes called the Seminal Indians.

"Anyway, back to the Young (pun on Jung?) Radishes. They are revolting against the Father Image of Uncle Sam, whom they both love and hate. Uncle is, of course, linked by

their subconsciouses with *unco*, a Scottish
word meaning strange, uncanny, weird, this
indicating that their own fathers were
strangers to them. All come from homes
where the father was missing or weak, a
phenomenon regrettably common in our culture.

"I never knew my own father . . . Tooney,
wipe that out as irrelevant. *Unco* also means
news or tidings, indicating that the unfortu-
nate young men are eagerly awaiting news
of the return of their fathers and perhaps
secretly hoping for reconciliation with Uncle
Sam, that is, their fathers.

"Uncle Sam. Sam is short for Samuel, from
the Hebrew *Shemu'el*, meaning Name of God.
All the Radishes are atheists, although some,
notably Omar Runic and Chibiabos Winnegan, were given religious instruction as
children (Panamorite and Roman Catholic,
respectively).

"Young Winnegan's revolt against God, and
against the Catholic Church, was undoubtedly
reinforced by the fact that his mother forced
strong *cath*artics upon him when he had a
chronic constipation. He probably also re-
sented having to learn his *cate*chism when
he preferred to play. And there is the deeply
significant and traumatic incident in which a
*cath*eter was used on him. (This refusal to
excrete when young will be analyzed in a later
report.)

"Uncle Sam, the Father Figure. *Figure* is so

obvious a play that I won't bother to point it out. Also perhaps on *figger*, in the sense of 'a fig on thee!'—look this up in Dante's *Inferno*, some Italian or other in Hell said, 'A fig on thee, God!' biting his thumb in the ancient gesture of defiance and disrespect. Hmm? Biting the thumb—an infantile characteristic?

"Sam is also a multileveled pun on phonetically, orthographically, and semisemantically linked words. It is significant that young Winnegan can't stand to be called *dear*; he claims that his mother called him that so many times it nauseates him. Yet the word has a deeper meaning to him. For instance, *sambar* is an Asiatic *deer* with *three*-pointed antlers. (Note the *sam*, also.) Obviously, the three points symbolize, to him, the Triple Revolution document, the historic dating point of the beginning of our era, which Chib claims to hate so. The three points are also archetypes of the Holy Trinity, which the Young Radishes frequently blaspheme against.

"I might point out that in this the group differs from others I've studied. The others expressed an infrequent and mild blasphemy in keeping with the mild, indeed pale, religious spirit prevalent nowadays. Strong blasphemers thrive only when strong believers thrive.

"Sam also stands for *same*, indicating the Radishes' subconscious desire to conform.

"Possibly, although this particular analysis

may be invalid, Sam corresponds to Samekh,
the fifteenth letter of the Hebrew alphabet.
(Sam! Ech!?) In the old style of English spell-
ing, which the Radishes learned in their childhood, the fifteenth letter of the Roman alphabet is O. In the Alphabet Table of my
dictionary, Webster's 128th New Collegiate,
the Roman O is in the same horizontal column
as the Arabic Dad. Also with the Hebrew
Mem. So we get a double connection with the
missing and longed for Father (or Dad) and
with the overdominating Mother (or Mem).

"I can make nothing out of the Greek Omicron, also in the same horizontal column. But
give me time; this takes study.

"Omicron. The little O! The lower-case omicron has an egg shape. The little egg is their
father's sperm fertilized? The womb? The
basic shape of modern architecture?

"Sam Hill, an archaic euphemism for Hell.
Uncle Sam is a Sam Hill of a father? Better
strike that out, Tooney. It's possible that
these highly educated youths have read about
this obsolete phrase, but it's not confirmable.
I don't want to suggest any connections that
might make me look ridiculous.

"Let's see. Samisen. A Japanese musical
instrument with *three* strings. The Triple
Revolution document and the Trinity again.
Trinity? Father, Son, and Holy Ghost. Mother
the thoroughly despised figure, hence, the
Wholly Goose? Well, maybe not. Wipe that
out, Tooney.

"Samisen. Son of Sam? Which leads naturally to Samson, who pulled down the temple of the Philistines on them and on himself. These boys talk of doing the same thing. Chuckle. Reminds me of myself when I was their age, before I matured. Strike out that last remark, Tooney.

"Samovar. The Russian word means, literally, self-boiler. There's no doubt the Radishes are boiling with revolutionary fervor. Yet their disturbed psyches know, deep down, that Uncle Sam is their everloving Father-Mother, that he has only their best interests at heart. But they force themselves to hate him, hence, they self-boil.

"A samlet is a young salmon. Cooked salmon is a yellowish pink or pale red, near to a radish in color, in their unconsciouses, anyway. Samlet equals Young Radish; they feel they're being cooked in the great pressure cooker of modern society.

"How's that for a trinely furned phase—I mean, finely turned phrase, Tooney? Run this off, edit as indicated, smooth it out, you know how, and send it off to the boss. I got to go. I'm late for lunch with Mother; she gets very upset if I'm not there on the dot.

"Oh, postscript! I recommend that the agents watch Winnegan more closely. His friends are blowing off psychic steam through talk and drink, but he has suddenly altered his behavior pattern. He has long periods of silence, he's given up smoking, drinking, and sex."

A PROFIT IS NOT WITHOUT HONOR

even in this day. The gummint has no overt
objection to privately owned taverns, run by
citizens who have paid all license fees, passed
all examinations, posted all bonds, and bribed
the local politicians and police chief. Since
there is no provision made for them, no large
buildings available for rent, the taverns are in
the homes of the owners themselves.

The Private Universe is Chib's favorite,
partly because the proprietor is operating
illegally. Dionysus Gobrinus, unable to hew
his way through the roadblocks, prise-de-
chevaux, barbed wire, and booby-traps of
official procedure, has quit his efforts to get a
license.

Openly, he paints the name of his establish-
ment over the mathematical equations that
once distinguished the exterior of the house.
(Math prof at Beverly Hills U. 14, named Al-
Khwarizmi Descartes Lobachevsky, he has
resigned and changed his name again.) The
atrium and several bedrooms have been converted for drinking and carousing. There are
no Egyptian customers, probably because of
their supersensitivity about the flowery
sentiments painted by patrons on the inside
walls.

**A BAS, ABU
MOHAMMED WAS THE SON OF A VIR-
GIN DOG
THE SPHINX STINKS
REMEMBER THE RED SEA!
THE PROPHET HAS A CAMEL FETISH**

Some of those who wrote the taunts have fathers, grandfathers, and great-grandfathers who were themselves the objects of similar insults. But their descendants are thoroughly assimilated, Beverly Hillsians to the core. Of such is the kingdom of men.

Gobrinus, a squat cube of a man, stands behind the bar, which is square as a protest against the ovoid. Above him is a big sign:

**ONE MAN'S MEAD IS ANOTHER MAN'S
POISSON**

Gobrinus has explained this pun many times, not always to his listener's satisfaction. Suffice it that Poisson was a mathematician and that Poisson's frequency distribution is a good approximation to the binomial distribution as the number of trials increases and probability of success in a single trial is small.

When a customer gets too drunk to be permitted one more drink, he is hurled headlong from the tavern with furious combustion and utter ruin by Gobrinus, who cries, "Poisson! Poisson!"

Chib's friends, the Young Radishes, sitting at a hexagonal table, greet him, and their words unconsciously echo those of the federal psycholinguist's estimate of his recent behavior.

"Chib, monk! Chibber as ever! Looking for a chibbie, no doubt! Take your pick!"

Madame Trismegista, sitting at a little table with a Seal-of-Solomon-shape top, greets him. She has been Gobrinus' wife for two years, a record, because she will knife him if he leaves her. Also, he believes that she can somehow juggle his destiny with the cards she deals. In this age of enlightenment, the soothsayer and astrologer flourish. As science pushes forward, ignorance and superstition gallop a-round the flanks and bite science in the rear with big dark teeth.

Gobrinus himself, a Ph.D., holder of the torch of knowledge (until lately, anyway), does not believe in God. But he is sure the stars are marching towards a baleful conjunction for him. With a strange logic, he thinks that his wife's cards control the stars; he is unaware that card-divination and astrology are entirely separate fields.

What can you expect of a man who claims that the universe is asymmetric?

Chib waves his hand at Madame Trismegista and walks to another table. Here sits

A TYPICAL TEEMAGER

Benedictine Serinus Melba. She is tall and slim and has narrow lemurlike hips and slender legs but big breasts. Her hair, black as the pupils of her eyes, is parted in the middle, plastered with perfumed spray to the skull, and braided into two long pigtails. These are brought over her bare shoulders and held together with a golden brooch just below her throat. From the brooch, which is in the form of a musical note, the braids part again, one looping under each breast. Another brooch secures them, and they separate to circle behind her back, are brooched again, and come back to meet on her belly. Another brooch holds them, and the twin waterfalls flow blackly over the front of her bell-shaped skirt.

Her face is thickly farded with green, aquamarine, a shamrock beauty mark, and topaz. She wears a yellow bra with artificial pink nipples; frilly lace ribbons hang from the bra. A demicorselet of bright green with black rosettes circles her waist. Over the corselet, half-concealing it, is a wire structure covered with a shimmering pink quilty material. It extends out in back to form a semifuselage or a bird's long tail, to which are attached long yellow and crimson artificial feathers.

An ankle-length diaphanous skirt billows out. It does not hide the yellow and dark-green striped lace-fringed garter-panties, white thighs, and black net stockings with green clocks in the shape of musical notes. Her shoes are bright blue with topaz high heels.

Benedictine is costumed to sing at the Folk Festival; the only thing missing is her singer's hat. Yet, she came to complain, among other things, that Chib has forced her to cancel her appearance and so lose her chance at a great career.

She is with five girls, all between sixteen and twenty-one, all drinking P (for popskull).

"Can't we talk in private, Benny?" Chib says.

"What for?" Her voice is a lovely contralto ugly with inflection.

"You got me down here to make a public scene," Chib says.

"For God's sake, what other kind of scene is there?" she shrills. "Look at him! He wants to talk to me alone!"

It is then that he realizes she is afraid to be alone with him. More than that, she is incapable of being alone. Now he knows why she insisted on leaving the bedroom door open with her girl-friend, Bela, within calling distance. And listening distance.

"You said you was just going to use your finger!" she shouts. She points at the slightly rounded belly. "I'm going to have a baby! You rotten smooth-talking sick bastard!"

"That isn't true at all," Chib says. "You told me it was all right, you loved me."

"'Love! Love!' he says! What the hell do I know what I said, you got me so excited! Anyway, I didn't say you could stick it in! I'd never say that, never! And then what you *did!* *What* you did! My God, I could hardly walk for a week, you bastard, you!"

Chib sweats. Except for Beethoven's Pastoral welling from the fido, the room is silent. His friends grin. Gobrinus, his back turned, is drinking scotch. Madame Trismegista shuffles her cards, and she farts with a fiery conjunction of beer and onions. Benedictine's friends look at their Mandarin-long fluorescent fingernails or glare at him. Her hurt and indignity is theirs and vice versa.

"I can't take those pills. They make me break out and give me eye trouble and screw up my monthlies! You know that! And I can't stand those mechanical uteruses! And you lied to me anyway! You said you took a pill!"

Chib realizes she's contradicting herself, but there's no use trying to be logical. She's furious because she's pregnant; she doesn't want to be inconvenienced with an abortion at this time, and she's out for revenge.

Now how, Chib wonders, how could she get pregnant *that* night? No woman, no matter how fertile, could have managed that. She must have been knocked up before or after. Yet she swears that it was that night, the night he was

THE KNIGHT OF THE BURNING PESTLE
OR
FOAM, FOAM ON THE RANGE

"No, no!" Benedictine cries.

"Why not? I love you," Chib says. "I want to marry you."

Benedictine screams, and her friend Bela, out in the hall, yells, "What's the matter? What happened?"

Benedictine does not reply. Raging, shaking as if in the grip of a fever, she scrambles out of bed, pushing Chib to one side. She runs to the small egg of the bathroom in the corner, and he follows her.

"I hope you're not going to do what I think . . .?" he says.

Benedictine moans, "You sneaky no-good son of a bitch!"

In the bathroom, she pulls down a section of wall, which becomes a shelf. On its top, attached by magnetic bottoms to the shelf, are many containers. She seizes a long thin can of spermatocide, squats, and inserts it. She presses the button on its bottom, and it foams with a hissing sound even its cover of flesh cannot silence.

Chib is paralyzed for a moment. Then he roars.

Benedictine shouts, "Stay away from me, you rude-ickle!"

From the door to the bedroom comes Bela's timid, "Are you all right, Benny?"

"I'll all-right her!" Chib bellows.

He jumps forward and takes a can of tempoxy glue from the shelf. The glue is used by Benedictine to attach her wigs to her head and will hold anything forever unless softened by a specific defixative.

Benedictine and Bela both cry out as Chib lifts Benedictine up and then lowers her to the floor. She fights, but he manages to spray the glue over the can and the skin and hairs around it.

"What're you doing?" she screams.

He pushes the button on the can to full-on position and then sprays the bottom with glue. While she struggles, he holds her arms tight against her body and keeps her from rolling over and so moving the can in or out. Silently, Chib counts to thirty, then to thirty more to make sure the glue is thoroughly dried. He releases her.

The foam is billowing out around her groin and down her legs and spreading out across the floor. The fluid in the can is under enormous pressure in the indestructible unpunchable can, and the foam expands vastly if exposed to open air.

Chib takes the can of defixative from the shelf and clutches it in his hand, determined that she will not have it. Benedictine jumps up

and swings at him. Laughing like a hyena in a
tentful of nitrous oxide, Chib blocks her fist
and shoves her away. Slipping on the foam,
which is ankle-deep by now. Benedictine falls
and then slides backward out of the bedroom
on her buttocks, the can clunking.

She gets to her feet and only then realizes
fully what Chib has done. Her scream goes up,
and she follows it. She dances around, yank-
ing at the can, her screams intensifying with
every tug and resultant pain. Then she turns
and runs out of the room or tries to. She
skids; Bela is in her way; they cling together
and both ski out of the room, doing a half-turn
while going through the door. The foam
swirls out so that the two look like Venus and
friend rising from the bubble-capped waves of
the Cyprian Sea.

Benedictine shoves Bela away but not
without losing some flesh to Bela's long sharp
fingernails. Bela shoots backwards through
the door toward Chib. She is like a novice ice
skater trying to maintain her balance. She
does not succeed and shoots by Chib, wailing,
on her back, her feet up in the air.

Chib slides his bare feet across the floor
gingerly, stops at the bed to pick up his
clothes, but decides he'd be wiser to wait until
he's outside before he puts them on. He gets
to the circular hall just in time to see Benedictine crawling past one of the columns that
divides the corridor from the atrium. Her parents, two middle-aged behemoths, are still sit-

ting on a flato, beer cans in hand, eyes wide,
mouths open, quivering.

Chib does not even say goodnight to them as
he passes along the hall. But then he sees
the fido and realizes that her parents had
switched it from EXT. to INT. and then to
Benedictine's room. Father and mother have
been watching Chib and daughter and it is evident from father's not-quite dwindled condition that father was very excited by this
show, superior to anything seen on exterior
fido.

"You peeping bastards!" Chib roars.

Benedictine has gotten to them and on her
feet and she is stammering, weeping, indicating the can and then stabbing her finger at
Chib. At Chib's roar, the parents heave up
from the flato as two leviathans from the
deep. Benedictine turns and starts to run
towards him, her arms outstretched, her long-
nailed fingers curved, her face a medusa's.
Behind her streams the wake of the livid
witch and father and mother on the foam.

Chib shoves up against a pillar and re-
bounds and skitters off, helpless to keep
himself from turning sidewise during the
maneuver. But he keeps his balance. Mama
and Papa have gone down together with a
crash that shakes even the solid house. They
are up, eyes rolling and bellowing like hippos
surfacing. They charge him but separate,
Mama shrieking now, her face, despite the fat,
Benedictine's. Papa goes around one side of

the pillar; Mama, the other. Benedictine has
rounded another pillar, holding to it with one
hand to keep her from slipping. She is between Chib and the door to the outside.

Chib slams against the wall of the corridor,
in an area free of foam. Benedictine runs
towards him. He dives across the floor, hits it,
and rolls between two pillars and out into the
atrium.

Mama and Papa converge in a collision
course. The Titanic meets the iceberg, and
both plunge swiftly. They skid on their faces
and bellies towards Benedictine. She leaps
into the air, trailing foam on them as they
pass beneath her.

By now it is evident that the government's
claim that the can is good for 40,000 shots of
death-to-sperm, or for 40,000 copulations, is
justified. Foam is all over the place ankle-
deep—knee-high in some places—and still
pouring out.

Bela is on her back now and on the atrium
floor, her head driven into the soft folds of the
flato.

Chib gets up slowly and stands for a
moment, glaring around him, his knees bent,
ready to jump from danger but hoping he
won't have to since his feet will undoubtedly
fly away from under him.

"Hold it, you rotten son of a bitch!" Papa
roars. "I'm going to kill you! You can't do this
to my daughter!"

Chib watches him turn over like a whale in

a heavy sea and try to get to his feet. Down he goes again, grunting as if hit by a harpoon. Mama is no more successful than he.

Seeing that his way is unbarred—Benedictine having disappeared somewhere—Chib skis across the atrium until he reaches an unfoamed area near the exit. Clothes over his arm, still holding the defixative, he struts towards the door.

At this moment Benedictine calls his name. He turns to see her sliding from the kitchen at him. In her hand is a tall glass. He wonders what she intends to do with it. Certainly, she is not offering him the hospitality of a drink.

Then she scoots into the dry region of the floor and topples forward with a scream. Nevertheless, she throws the contents of the glass accurately.

Chib screams when he feels the boiling hot water, painful as if he had been circumcised unanesthetized.

Benedictine, on the floor, laughs. Chib, after jumping around and shrieking, the can and clothes dropped, his hands holding the scalded parts, manages to control himself. He stops his antics, seizes Benedictine's right hand, and drags her out into the streets of Beverly Hills. There are quite a few people out this night, and they follow the two. Not until Chib reaches the lake does he stop and there he goes into the water to cool off the burn, Benedictine with him.

The crowd has much to talk about later,

after Benedictine and Chib have crawled out of the lake and then run home. The crowd talks and laughs quite a while as they watch the sanitation department people clean the foam off the lake surface and the streets.

"I was so sore I couldn't walk for a month!" Benedictine screams.

"You had it coming," Chib says. "You've got no complaints. You said you wanted my baby, and you talked as if you meant it."

"I must've been out of mind!" Benedictine says. "No, I wasn't! I never said no such thing! You lied to me! You forced me!"

"I would never force anybody," Chib said. "You know that. Quit your bitching. You're a free agent, and you consented freely. You have free will."

Omar Runic, the poet, stands up from his chair. He is a tall thin red-bronze youth with an aquiline nose and very thick red lips. His kinky hair grows long and is cut into the shape of the *Pequod*, that fabled vessel which bore mad Captain Ahab and his mad crew and the sole survivor Ishmael after the white whale. The coiffure is formed with a bowsprit and hull and three masts and yardarms and even a boat hanging on davits.

Omar Runic claps his hands and shouts, "Bravo! A philosopher! Free will it is; free will to seek the Eternal Verities—if any—or Death and Damnation! I'll drink to free will! A toast, gentlemen! Stand up, Young Radishes,

a toast to our leader!"
    And so begins

THE MAD P PARTY

    Madame Trismegista calls, "Tell your fortune, Chib! See what the stars tell through the cards!"
    He sits down at her table while his friends crowd around.
    "O.K., Madame. How do I get out of this mess?"
    She shuffles and turns over the top card.
    "Jesus! The ace of spades!"
    "You're going on a long journey!"
    "Egypt!" Rousseau Red Hawk cries. "Oh, no, you don't want to go there, Chib! Come with me to where the buffalo roam and . . ."
    Up comes another card.
    "You will soon meet a beautiful dark lady."
    "A goddam Arab! Oh, no, Chib, tell me it's not true!"
    "You will win great honors soon."
    "Chib's going to get the grant!"
    "If I get the grant, I don't have to go to Egypt," Chib says. "Madame Trismegista, with all due respect, you're full of crap."
    "Don't mock, young man. I'm not a computer. I'm tuned to the spectrum of psychic vibrations."

Flip. "You will be in great danger, physically and morally."

Chib says, "That happens at least once a day."

Flip. "A man very close to you will die twice."

Chib pales, rallies, and says, "A coward dies a thousand deaths."

"You will travel in time, return to the past."

"Zow!" Red Hawk says. "You're outdoing yourself, Madame. Careful! You'll get a psychic hernia, have to wear an ectoplasmic truss!"

"Scoff if you want to, you dumbshits," Madame says. "There are more worlds than one. The cards don't lie, not when I deal them."

"Gobrinus!" Chib calls. "Another pitcher of beer for the Madame."

The young Radishes return to their table, a legless disc held up in the air by a graviton field. Benedictine glares at them and goes into a huddle with the other teemagers. At a table nearby sits Pinkerton Legrand, a gummint agent, facing them so that the fido under his one-way window of a jacket beams in on them. They know he's doing this. He knows they know and has reported so to his superior. He frowns when he sees Falco Accipiter enter. Legrand does not like an agent from another department messing around on his case. Accipiter does not even look at Legrand. He orders a pot of tea and then pretends to drop into the teapot a pill that combines with tannic acid to become P.

Rousseau Red Hawk winks at Chib and says, "Do you really think it's possible to paralyze all of LA with a single bomb?"

"Three bombs!" Chib says loudly so that Legrand's fido will pick up the words. "One for the control console of the desalinization plant, a second for the backup console, the third for the nexus of the big pipe that carries the water to the reservoir on the 20th level."

Pinkerton Legrand turns pale. He downs all the whiskey in his glass and orders another, although he has already had too many. He presses the plate on his fido to transmit a triple top-priority. Lights blink redly in HQ; a gong clangs repeatedly; the chief wakes up so suddenly he falls off his chair.

Accipiter also hears, but he sits stiff, dark, and brooding as the diorite image of a Pharaoh's falcon. Monomaniac, he is not to be diverted by talk of inundating all LA, even if it will lead to action. On Grandpa's trail, he is now here because he hopes to use Chib as the key to the house. One "mouse"—as he thinks of his criminals—one "mouse" will run to the hole of another.

"When do you think we can go into action?" Huga Wells-Erb Heinsturbury, the science-fiction authoress, says.

"In about three weeks," Chib says.

At HQ, the chief curses Legrand for disturbing him. There are thousands of young men and women blowing off steam with these plots of destruction, assassination, and revolt. He does not understand why the young punks talk like this, since they have everything handed them free. If he had his way, he'd throw them into jail and kick them around a little or more than.

"After we do it, we'll have to take off for the big outdoors," Red Hawk says. His eyes glisten. "I'm telling you, boys, being a free man in the forest is the greatest. You're a genuine individual, not just one of the faceless breed."

Red Hawk believes in this plot to destroy LA. He is happy because, though he hasn't said so, he has grieved while in Mother Nature's lap for intellectual companionship. The other savages can hear a deer at a hundred yards, detect a rattlesnake in the bushes, but they're deaf to the footfalls of philosophy, the neigh of Nietzsche, the rattle of Russell, the honkings of Hegel.

"The illiterate swine!" he says aloud. The others say, "What?"

"Nothing. Listen, you guys must know how wonderful it is. You were in the WNRCC."

"I was 4-F," Omar Runic says. "I got hay fever."

"I was working on my second M.A.," Gibbon Tacitus says.

"I was in the WNRCC band," Sibelius Amadeus Yehudi says. "We only got outside when we played the camps, and that wasn't often."

"Chib, you were in the Corps. You loved it, didn't you?"

Chib nods but says, "Being a neo-Amerind takes all your time just to survive. When could I paint? And who would see the paintings if I did get time? Anyway, that's no life for a woman or a baby."

Red Hawk looks hurt and orders a whiskey mixed with P.

Pinkerton Legrand doesn't want to interrupt his monitoring, yet he can't stand the pressure in his bladder. He walks towards the room used as the customers' catch-all. Red Hawk, in a nasty mood caused by rejection, sticks his leg out. Legrand trips, catches himself, and stumbles forward. Benedictine puts out her leg. Legrand falls on his face. He no longer has any reason to go to the urinal except to wash himself off.

Everybody except Legrand and Accipiter laugh. Legrand jumps up, his fists doubled. Benedictine ignores him and walks over to Chib, her friends following. Chib stiffens. She says, "You perverted bastard! You told me you were just going to use your finger!"

"You're repeating yourself," Chib says. "The important thing is, what's going to happen to the baby?"

"What do you care?" Benedictine says. "For all you know, it might not even be yours!"

"That'd be a relief," Chib says, "if it weren't. Even so, the baby should have a say in this. He might want to live—even with you as his mother."

"In this miserable life!" she cries. "I'm
going to do it a favor. I'm going to the hospital
and get rid of it. Because of you, I have to miss
out on my big chance at the Folk Festival!
There'll be agents from all over there, and I
won't get a chance to sing for them!"

"You're a liar," Chib says. "You're all
dressed up to sing."

Benedictine's face is red; her eyes, wide; her
nostrils, flaring.

"You spoiled my fun!"

She shouts, "Hey, everybody, want to hear a
howler! This great artist, this big hunk of
manhood, Chib the divine, he can't get a
hard-on unless he's gone down on!"

Chib's friends look at each other. What's
the bitch screaming about? So what's new?

From Grandpa's *Private Ejaculations:* Some
of the features of the Panamorite religion, so
reviled and loathed in the 21st century, have
become everyday facts in modern times. Love,
love, love, physical and spiritual! It's not
enough to just kiss your children and hug
them. But oral stimulation of the genitals of
infants by the parents and relatives has re-
sulted in some curious conditioned reflexes. I
could write a book about this aspect of mid-
22nd century life and probably will.

Legrand comes out of the washroom. Benedictine slaps Chib's face. Chib slaps her back.

Gobrinus lifts up a section of the bar and hurtles through the opening, crying, "Poisson! Poisson!"

He collides with Legrand, who lurches into Bela, who screams, whirls, and slaps Legrand, who slaps back. Benedictine empties a glass of P in Chib's face. Howling, he jumps up and swings his fist. Benedictine ducks, and the fist goes over her shoulder into a girl-friend's chest.

Red Hawk leaps up on the table and shouts, "I'm a regular bearcat, half-alligator and half . . ."

The table, held up in a graviton field, can't bear much weight. It tilts and catapults him into the girls, and all go down. They bite and scratch Red Hawk, and Benedictine squeezes his testicles. He screams, writhes, and hurls Benedictine with his feet onto the top of the table. It has regained its normal height and altitude, but now it flips over again, tossing her to the other side. Legrand, tippytoeing through the crowd on his way to the exit, is knocked down. He loses some front teeth against somebody's knee cap. Spitting blood and teeth, he jumps up and slugs a bystander.

Gobrinus fires off a gun that shoots a tiny Very light. It's supposed to blind the brawlers and so bring them to their senses while they're regaining their sight. It hangs in the air and shines like

A STAR OVER BEDLAM

The Police Chief is talking via fido to a man in a public booth. The man has turned off the video and is disguising his voice.

"They're beating the shit out of each other in The Private Universe."

The Chief groans. The Festival has just begun, and They are at it already.

"Thanks. The boys'll be on the way. What's your name? I'd like to recommend you for a Citizen's Medal."

"What! And get the shit knocked out of me, too! I ain't no stoolie; just doing my duty. Besides, I don't like Gobrinus or his customers. They're a bunch of snobs."

The Chief issues orders to the riot squad, leans back, and drinks a beer while he watches the operation on fido. What's the matter with these people, anyway? They're always mad about something.

The sirens scream. Although the bolgani ride electrically driven noiseless tricycles, they're still clinging to the centuries-old tradition of warning the criminals that they're coming. Five trikes pull up before the open door of The Private Universe. The police dismount and confer. Their two-storied cylindrical helmets are black and have scarlet roaches. They wear goggles for some reason although their vehicles can't go over 15 m.p.h. Their jackets are black and fuzzy, like a teddy bear's fur, and huge golden epaulets decorate their shoulders. The shorts are electric-blue and fuzzy; the jackboots, glossy black. They carry electric shock sticks and guns that fire chokegas pellets.

Gobrinus blocks the entrance. Sergeant O'Hara says, "Come on, let us in. No, I don't have a warrant of entry. But I'll get one."

"If you do, I'll sue," Gobrinus says. He smiles. While it is true that government red tape was so tangled he quit trying to acquire a tavern legally, it is also true that the government will protect him in this issue. Invasion of privacy is a tough rap for the police to break.

O'Hara looks inside the doorway at the two bodies on the floor, at those holding their heads and sides and wiping off blood, and at Accipiter, sitting like a vulture dreaming of carrion. One of the bodies gets up on all fours and crawls through between Gobrinus' legs out into the street.

"Sergeant, arrest that man!" Gobrinus says. "He's wearing an illegal fido. I accuse him of invasion of privacy."

O'Hara's face lights up. At least he'll get one arrest to his credit. Legrand is placed in the paddywagon, which arrives just after the ambulance. Red Hawk is carried out as far as the doorway by his friends. He opens his eyes just as he's being carried on a stretcher to the ambulance and he mutters.

O'Hara leans over him. "What?"

"I fought a bear once with only my knife, and I came out better than with those cunts. I charge them with assault and battery, murder and mayhem."

O'Hara's attempt to get Red Hawk to sign a warrant fails because Red Hawk is now unconscious. He curses. By the time Red Hawk begins feeling better, he'll refuse to sign the warrant. He won't want the girls and their boy-friends laying for him, not if he has any sense at all.

Through the barred window of the paddy-wagon, Legrand screams, "I'm a gummint agent! You can't arrest me!"

The police get a hurry-up call to go to the front of the Folk Center, where a fight between local youths and Westwood invaders is threatening to become a riot. Benedictine leaves the tavern. Despite several blows in the shoulders and stomach, a kick in the buttocks, and a bang on the head, she shows no sign of losing the fetus.

Chib, half-sad, half-glad, watches her go. He feels a dull grief that the baby is to be denied life. By now he realizes that part of his objection to the abortion is identification with the fetus; he knows what Grandpa thinks he does not know. He realizes that his birth was an accident—lucky or unlucky. If things had gone otherwise, he would not have been born. The thought of his nonexistence—no painting,

no friends, no laughter, no hope, no love—
horrifies him. His mother, drunkenly negli-
gent about contraception, has had any number of abortions, and he could have been one
of them.

Watching Benedictine swagger away (despite her torn clothes), he wonders what he
could ever have seen in her. Life with her,
even with a child, would have been gritty.

In the hope-lined nest of the mouth
Love flies once more, nestles down,
Coos, flashes feathered glory, dazzles,
And then flies away, crapping,
As is the wont of birds,
To jet-assist the take off.

—Omar Runic

Chib returns to his home, but he still can't
get back into his room. He goes to the storeroom. The painting is seven-eighths finished
but was not completed because he was dis-
satisfied with it. Now he takes it from the
house and carries it to Runic's house, which is
in the same clutch as his. Runic is at the
Center, but he always leaves his doors open
when he's gone. He has equipment which Chib
uses to finish the painting, working with a
sureness and intensity he lacked the first time
he was creating it. He then leaves Runic's
house with the huge oval canvas held above
his head.

He strides past the pedestals and under
their curving branches with the ovoids at
their ends. He skirts several small grassy
parks with trees, walks beneath more houses,
and in ten minutes is nearing the heart of
Beverly Hills. Here mercurial Chib sees

ALL IN THE GOLDEN AFTERNOON, THREE LEADEN LADIES

drifting in a canoe on Lake Issus. Maryam
bint Yusuf, her mother, and aunt listlessly
hold fishing poles and look towards the gay
colors, music, and the chattering crowd before the Folk Center. By now the police have
broken up the juvenile fight and are standing
around to make sure nobody else makes
trouble.

The three women are dressed in the somber
clothes, completely body-concealing, of the
Mohammedan Wahhabi fundamentalist sect.
They do not wear veils; not even the Wahhabi
now insist on this. Their Egyptian brethren
ashore are clad in modern garments, shame-
ful and sinful. Despite which, the ladies stare
at them.

Their menfolk are at the edge of the crowd.
Bearded and costumed like sheiks in a Foreign Legion fido show, they mutter gargling

oaths and hiss at the iniquitous display of
female flesh. But they stare.

This small group has come from the zoological preserves of Abyssinia, where they
were caught poaching. Their gummint gave
them three choices. Imprisonment in a rehabilitation center, where they would be
treated until they became good citizens if it
took the rest of their lives. Emigration to the
megalopolis of Haifa, Israel. Or emigration to
Beverly Hills, LA.

What, dwell among the accursed Jews of
Israel? They spat and chose Beverly Hills.
Alas, Allah had mocked them! They were
now surrounded by Finkelsteins, Applebaums,
Siegels, Weintraubs, and others of the infidel
tribes of Isaac. Even worse, Beverly Hills had
no mosque. They either traveled forty kilometers every day to the 16th level, where a
mosque was available, or used a private
home.

Chib hastens to the edge of the plastic-
edged lake and puts down his painting and
bows low, whipping off his somewhat bat-
tered hat. Maryam smiles at him but loses the
smile when the two chaperones reprimand
her.

"Ya kelb! Ya ibn kelb!" the two shout at
him.

Chib grins at them, waves his hat, and says,
"Charmed, I'm sure, mesdames! Oh, you
lovely ladies remind me of the Three Graces."

He then cries out, "I love you, Maryam! I

love you! Thou art like the Rose of Sharon to me! Beautiful, doe-eyed, virginal! A fortress of innocence and strength, filled with a fierce motherhood and utter faithfulness to the one true love! I love thee, thou art the only light in a black sky of dead stars! I cry to you across the void!"

Maryam understands World English, but the wind carries his words away from her. She simpers, and Chib cannot help feeling a momentary repulsion, a flash of anger as if she has somehow betrayed him. Nevertheless, he rallies and shouts, "I invite you to come with me to the showing! You and your mother and aunt will be my guests. You can see my paintings, my soul, and know what kind of man is going to carry you off on his Pegasus, my dove!"

There is nothing as ridiculous as the verbal outpourings of a young poet in love. Outrageously exaggerated. I laugh. But I am also touched. Old as I am, I remember my first loves, the fires, the torrents of words, lightning-sheathed, ache-winged. Dear lasses, most of you are dead; the rest, withered. I blow you a kiss.

—Grandpa

Maryam's mother stands up in the canoe. For a second, her profile is to Chib, and he sees intimations of the hawk that Maryam will be when she is her mother's age. Maryam now has a gently aquiline face—"the sweep of the sword of love"—Chib has called that nose. Bold but beautiful. However, her mother does look like a dirty old eagle. And her aunt—uneaglish but something of the camel in those features.

Chib suppresses the unfavorable, even treacherous, comparisons. But he cannot suppress the three bearded, robed, and unwashed men who gather around him.

Chib smiles but says, "I don't remember inviting you."

They look blank since rapidly spoken LA English is a huftymagufty to them. Abu—generic name for any Egyptian in Beverly Hills—rasps an oath so ancient even the pre-Mohammed Meccans knew it. He forms a fist. Another Arab steps towards the painting and draws back a foot as if to kick it.

At this moment, Maryam's mother discovers that it is as dangerous to stand in a canoe as on a camel. It is worse, because the three women cannot swim.

Neither can the middle-aged Arab who attacks Chib, only to find his victim sidestepping and then urging him on into the lake with a foot in the rear. One of the young men rushes Chib; the other starts to kick at the painting. Both halt on hearing the three women scream and on seeing them go over into the water.

Then the two run to the edge of the lake,

where they also go into the water, propelled
by one of Chib's hands in each of their backs.
A bolgan hears the six of them screaming and
thrashing around and runs over to Chib. Chib
is becoming concerned because Maryam is
having trouble staying above the water. Her
terror is not faked.

What Chib does not understand is why they
are all carrying on so. Their feet must be on
the bottom; the surface is below their chins.
Despite which, Maryam looks as if she is
going to drown. So do the others, but he is not
interested in them. He should go in after
Maryam. However, if he does, he will have to
get a change of clothes before going to the
showing.

At this thought, he laughs loudly and then
even more loudly as the bolgan goes in after
the women. He picks up the painting and
walks off laughing. Before he reaches the
Center, he sobers.

"Now, how come Grandpa was so right?
How does he read me so well? Am I fickle, too
shallow? No, I have been too deeply in love
too many times. Can I help it if I love Beauty,
and the beauties I love do not have enough
Beauty? My eye is too demanding; it cancels
the urgings of my heart."

THE MASSACRE OF THE INNER SENSE

The entrance hall (one of twelve) which Chib enters was designed by Grandpa Winnegan. The visitor comes into a long curving tube lined with mirrors at various angles. He sees a triangular door at the end of the corridor. The door seems to be too tiny for anybody over nine years old to enter. The illusion makes the visitor feel as if he's walking up the wall as he progresses towards the door. At the end of the tube, the visitor is convinced he's standing on the ceiling.

But the door gets larger as he approaches until it becomes huge. Commentators have guessed that this entrance is the architect's symbolic representation of the gateway to the world of art. One should stand on his head before entering the wonderland of aesthetics.

On going in, the visitor thinks at first that the tremendous room is inside out or reversed. He gets even dizzier. The far wall actually seems the near wall until the visitor gets reorientated. Some people can't adjust and have to get out before they faint or vomit.

On the right hand is a hatrack with a sign: HANG YOUR HEAD HERE. A double pun by Grandpa, who always carries a joke too far for most people. If Grandpa goes beyond the bounds of verbal good taste, his great-great-grandson has overshot the moon in his paintings. Thirty of his latest have been revealed, including the last three of his Dog Series: *Dog Star, Dog Would* and *Dog Tiered.* Ruskinson and his disciples are threatening to throw up. Luscus and his flock praise, but they're restrained. Luscus has told them to wait until he talks to young Winnegan before they go all-out. The fido men are busy shooting and interviewing both and trying to provoke a quarrel.

The main room of the building is a huge hemisphere with a bright ceiling which runs through the complete spectrum every nine minutes. The floor is a giant chessboard, and in the center of each square is a face, each of a great in the various arts. Michelangelo, Mozart, Balzac, Zeuxis, Beethoven, Li Po, Twain, Dostoyevsky Farmisto, Mbuzi, Cupel, Krishnagurti, etc. Ten squares are left face-less so that future generations may add their own nominees for immortality.

The lower part of the wall is painted with murals depicting significant events in the lives of the artists. Against the curving wall are nine stages, one for each of the Muses. On a console above each stage is a giant statue of the presiding goddess. They are naked and have overripe figures: huge-breasted, broad-hipped, sturdy-legged, as if the sculptor thought of them as Earth goddesses, not refined intellectual types.

The faces are basically structured like the

smooth placid faces of classical Greek sta-
tues, but they have an unsettling expression around the mouths and eyes. The lips
are smiling but seem ready to break into
a snarl. The eyes are deep and menacing.
DON'T SELL ME OUT, they say. IF YOU
DO . . .

A transparent plastic hemisphere extends
over each stage and has acoustic properties
which keep people who are not beneath the
shell from hearing the sounds emanating
from the stage and vice versa.

Chib makes his way through the noisy
crowd towards the stage of Polyhymnia, the
Muse who includes painting in her province.
He passes the stage on which Benedictine is
standing and pouring her lead heart out in an
alchemy of golden notes. She sees Chib and
manages somehow to glare at him and at the
same time to keep smiling at her audience.
Chib ignores her but observes that she has
replaced the dress ripped in the tavern. He
sees also the many policemen stationed
around the building. The crowd does not seem
in an explosive mood. Indeed, it seems happy,
if boisterous. But the police know how decep-
tive this can be. One spark . . .

Chib goes by the stage of Calliope, where
Omar Runic is extemporizing. He comes to
Polyhymnia's, nods at Rex Luscus, who waves
at him, and sets his painting on the stage. It is
titled *The Massacre of the Innocents* (subtitle:
Dog in the Manger).

The painting depicts a stable.

The stable is a grotto with curiously shaped stalactites. The light that breaks—or fractures—through the cave is Chib's red. It penetrates every object, doubles its strength, and then rays out jaggedly. The viewer, moving from side to side to get a complete look, can actually see the many levels of light as he moves, and thus he catches glimpses of the figures under the exterior figures.

The cows, sheep, and horses are in stalls at the end of the cave. Some are looking with horror at Mary and the infant. Others have their mouths open, evidently trying to warn Mary. Chib has used the legend that the animals in the manager were able to talk to each other the night Christ was born.

Joseph, a tired old man, so slumped he seems back-boneless, is in a corner. He wears two horns, but each has a halo, so it's all right.

Mary's back is to the bed of straw on which the infant is supposed to be. From a trapdoor in the floor of the cave, a man is reaching to place a huge egg on the straw bed. He is in a cave beneath the cave and is dressed in modern clothes, has a boozy expression, and, like Joseph, slumps as if invertebrate. Behind him a grossly fat woman, looking remarkably like Chib's mother, has the baby, which the man passed on to her before putting the foundling egg on the straw bed.

The baby has an exquisitely beautiful face and is suffused with a white glow from his halo. The woman has removed the halo from his head and is using the sharp edge to butcher the baby.

Chib has a deep knowledge of anatomy, since he has dissected many corpses while getting his Ph.D. in art at Beverly Hills U. The body of the infant is not unnaturally elongated, as so many of Chib's figures are. It is more than photographic; it seems to be an actual baby. Its viscera is unraveled through a large bloody hole.

The onlookers are struck in their viscera as if this were not a painting but a real infant, slashed and disemboweled, found on their doorsteps as they left home.

The egg has a semitransparent shell. In its murky yolk floats a hideous little devil, horns, hooves, tail. Its blurred features resemble a combination of Henry Ford's and Uncle Sam's. When the viewers shift to one side or the other, the faces of others appear: prominents in the development of modern society.

The window is crowded with wild animals that have come to adore but have stayed to scream soundlessly in horror. The beasts in the foreground are those that have been exterminated by man or survive only in zoos and natural preserves. The dodo, the blue whale, the passenger pigeon, the quagga, the gorilla, orangutan, polar bear, cougar, lion, tiger, grizzly bear, California condor, kangaroo, wombat, rhinoceros, bald eagle.

Behind them are other animals and, on a

hill, the dark crouching shapes of the Tasmanian aborigine and Haitian Indian.

"What is your considered opinion of this rather remarkable painting, Doctor Luscus?" a fido interviewer asks.

Luscus smiles and says, "I'll have a considered judgment in a few minutes. Perhaps you'd better talk to Doctor Ruskinson first. He seems to have made up his mind at once. Fools and angels, you know."

Ruskinson's red face and scream of fury are transmitted over the fido.

"The shit heard around the world!" Chib says loudly.

"INSULT! SPITTLE! PLASTIC DUNG! A BLOW IN THE FACE OF ART AND A KICK IN THE BUTT FOR HUMANITY! INSULT! INSULT!"

"Why is it such an insult, Doctor Ruskinson?" the fido man says. "Because it mocks the Christian faith, and also the Panamorite faith? It doesn't seem to me it does that. It seems to me that Winnegan is trying to say that men have perverted Christianity, maybe all religions, all ideals, for their own greedy self-destructive purposes, that man is basically a killer and a perverter. At least, that's what I get out of it, although of course I'm only a simple layman, and . . ."

"Let the critics make the analysis, young man!" Ruskinson snaps. "Do you have a double Ph.D., one in psychiatry and one in art? Have you been certified as a critic by the government?

"Winnegan, who has no talent whatsoever, let alone this genius that various self-deluded blowhards prate about, this abomination from Beverly Hills, presents his junk—actually a mishmash which has attracted attention solely because of a new technique that any electronic technician could invent—I am enraged that a mere gimmick, a trifling novelty, can not only fool certain sectors of the public but highly educated and federally certified critics such as Doctor Luscus here—although there will always be scholarly asses who bray so loudly, pompously, and obscurely that . . ."

"Isn't it true," the fido man says, "that many painters we now call great, Van Gogh for one, were condemned or ignored by their contemporary critics? And . . ."

The fido man, skilled in provoking anger for the benefit of his viewers, pauses. Ruskinson swells, his head a bloodvessel just before aneurysm.

"I'm no ignorant layman!" he screams. "I can't help it that there have been Luscuses in the past! I know what I'm talking about! Winnegan is only a micrometeorite in the heaven of Art, not fit to shine the shoes of the great luminaries of painting. His reputation has been pumped up by a certain clique so it can shine in the reflected glory, the hyenas, biting the hand that feeds them, like mad dogs . . ."

"Aren't you mixing your metaphors a little bit?" the fido man says.

Luscus takes Chib's hand tenderly and draws him to one side where they're out of fido range.

"Darling Chib," he coos, "now is the time to declare yourself. You know how vastly I love you, not only as an artist but for yourself. It must be impossible for you to resist any longer the deeply sympathetic vibrations that leap unhindered between us. God, if you only knew how I dreamed of you, my glorious godlike Chib, with . . ."

"If you think I'm going to say yes because you have the power to make or break my reputation, to deny me the grant, you're wrong," Chib says. He jerks his hand away.

Luscus' good eye glares. He says, "Do you find me repulsive? Surely it can't be on moral grounds . . ."

"It's the principle of the thing," Chib says. "Even if I were in love with you, which I'm not, I wouldn't let you make love to me. I want to be judged on my merit alone, that only. Come to think of it, I don't give a damn about anybody's judgment. I don't want to hear praise or blame from you or anybody. Look at my paintings and talk to each other, you jackals. But don't try to make me agree with your little images of me."

THE ONLY GOOD CRITIC IS A DEAD CRITIC

Omar Runic has left his dais and now stands before Chib's paintings. He places one hand on his naked left chest, on which is tattooed the face of Herman Melville, Homer occupying the other place of honor on his right breast. He shouts loudly, his black eyes like furnace doors blown out by explosion. As has happened before, he is seized with inspiration derived from Chib's paintings.

"Call me Ahab, not Ishmael.
For I have hooked the Leviathan.
I am the wild ass's colt born to a man.
Lo, my eye has seen it all!
My bosom is like wine that has no vent.
I am a sea with doors, but the doors are
 stuck.
Watch out! The skin will burst; the doors
 will break.

"You are Nimrod, I say to my friend,
 Chib.
And now is the hour when God says to his
 angels,
If this is what he can do as a beginning,
 then
Nothing is impossible for him.
He will be blowing his horn before

The ramparts of Heaven and shouting for
The Moon as hostage, the Virgin as wife,
And demanding a cut on the profits
From the Great Whore of Babylon."

"Stop that son of a bitch!" the Festival
Director shouts. "He'll cause a riot like he did
last year!"

The bolgani begin to move in. Chib watches
Luscus, who is talking to the fido man. Chib
can't hear Luscus, but he's sure Luscus is not
saying complimentary things about him.

"Melville wrote of me long before I was
    born.
I'm the man who wants to comprehend
The Universe but comprehend on my
    terms.
I am Ahab whose hate must pierce,
    shatter,
All impediment of Time, Space, or
    Subject
Mortality and hurl my fierce
Incandescence into the Womb of
    Creation,
Disturbing in its Lair whatever Force or
Unknown Thing-in-Itself crouches there,
Remote, removed, unrevealed."

The Director gestures at the police to
remove Runic. Ruskinson is still shouting, although the cameras are pointing at Runic or
Luscus. One of the Young Radishes, Huga

Wells-Erb Heinsturbury, the science-fiction authoress, is shaking with hysteria generated by Runic's voice and with a lust for revenge. She is sneaking up on a *Time* fido man. *Time* has long ago ceased to be a magazine, since there are no magazines, but became a government-supported communications bureau. *Time* is an example of Uncle Sam's left-hand, right-hand, hands-off policy of providing communications bureaus with all they need and at the same time permitting the bureau executives to determine the bureau policies. Thus, government provision and free speech are united. This is fine, in theory, anyway.

Time has revived several of its original policies, that is, truth and objectivity must be sacrificed for the sake of a witticism and science-fiction must be put down. *Time* has sneered at every one of Heinsturbury's works, and so she is out to get some personal satisfaction for the hurt caused by the unfair reviews.

> "*Quid nunc? Cui bono?*
> Time? Space? Substance? Accident?
> When you die—Hell? Nirvana?
> Nothing is nothing to think about.
> The canons of philosophy boom.
> Their projectiles are duds.
> The ammo heaps of theology blow up,
> Set off by the saboteur Reason.

"Call me Ephraim, for I was halted
At the Ford of God and could not tongue
The sibilance to let me pass.
Well, I can't pronounce shibboleth,
But I can say shit!"

Huga Wells-Erb Heinsturbury kicks the
Time fido man in the balls. He throws up his
hands, and the football-shaped, football-sized
camera sails from his hands and strikes a
youth on the head. The youth is a Young
Radish, Ludwig Euterpe Mahlzart. He is smol-
dering with rage because of the damnation of
his tone poem, *Jetting The Stuff Of Future
Hells*, and the camera is the extra fuel needed
to make him blaze up uncontrollably. He
punches the chief musical critic in his fat
belly.

Huga, not the *Time* man, is screaming with
pain. Her bare toes have struck the hard
plastic armor with which the *Time* man,
recipient of many such a kick, protects his
genitals. Huga hops around on one foot while
holding the injured foot in her hands. She
twirls into a girl, and there is a chain effect. A
man falls against the *Time* man, who is stooping over to pick up his camera.

"Ahaaa!" Huga screams and tears off the
Time man's helmet and straddles him and
beats him over the head with the optical end
of the camera. Since the solid-state camera
is still working, it is sending to billions of
viewers some very intriguing, if dizzying, pic-

tures. Blood obscures one side of the picture, but not so much that the viewers are wholly cheated. And then they get another novel shot as the camera flies into the air again, turning over and over.

A bolgan has shoved his shock-stick against her back, causing her to stiffen and propel the camera in a high arc behind her. Huga's current lover grapples with the bolgan; they roll on the floor; a Westwood juvenile picks up the shock-stick and has a fine time goosing the adults around him until a local youth jumps him.

"Riots are the opium of the people," the Police Chief groans. He calls in all units and puts in a call to the Chief of Police of Westwood, who is, however, having his own troubles.

Runic beats his breast and howls.

> "Sir, I exist! And don't tell me,
> As you did Crane, that that creates
> No obligation in you towards me.
> I am a man; I am unique.
> I've thrown the Bread out the window,
> Pissed in the Wine, pulled the plug
> From the bottom of the Ark, cut the Tree
> For firewood, and if there were a Holy
> Ghost, I'd goose him.
> But I know that it all does not mean
> A God damned thing.
> That nothing means nothing,
> That is is is and not-is not is is-not

That a rose is a rose is a
That we are here and will not be
And that is all we can know!"

Ruskinson sees Chib coming towards him,
squawks, and tries to escape. Chib seizes the
canvas of *Dogmas from a Dog* and batters
Ruskinson over the head with it. Luscus
protests in horror, not because of the damage
done to Ruskinson but because the painting
might be damaged. Chib turns around and
batters Luscus in the stomach with the oval's
edge.

"The earth lurches like a ship going
   down,
Its back almost broken by the flood of
Excrement from the heavens and the
   deeps,
What God in His terrible munificence
Has granted on hearing Ahab cry,
Bullshit! Bullshit!

"I weep to think that this is Man
And this his end. But wait!
On the crest of the flood, a three-master
Of antique shape. The Flying Dutchman!
And Ahab is astride a ship's deck once
   more.
Laugh, you Fates, and mock, you Norns!
For I am Ahab and I am Man,
And though I cannot break a hole
through the wall of What Seems

To grab a handful of What Is,
Yet, I will keep on punching.
And I and my crew will not give up,
Though the timbers split beneath our feet
And we sink to become indistinguishable
From the general excrement.

"For a moment that will burn on the
Eye of God forever, Ahab stands
Outlined against the blaze of Orion,
Fist clenched, a bloody phallus,
Like Zeus exhibiting the trophy of
The unmanning of his father Cronus.
And then he and his crew and ship
Dip and hurtle headlong over
The edge of the world.
And from what I hear, they are still

F
a
l
l
i
n
g"

   Chib is shocked into a quivering mass by a
jolt from a bolgan's electrical riot stick. While
he is recovering, he hears his Grandpa's voice
issuing from the transceiver in his hat.
   "Chib, come quick! Accipiter has broken in
and is trying to get through the door of my
room!"
   Chib gets up and fights and shoves his way

to the exit. When he arrives, panting, at his home he finds that the door to Grandpa's room has been opened. The IRB men and electronic technicians are standing in the hallway. Chib bursts into Grandpa's room. Accipiter is standing in its middle and quivering and pale. Nervous stone. He sees Chib and shrinks back, saying, "It wasn't my fault. I had to break in. It was the only way I could find out for sure. It wasn't my fault; I didn't touch him."

Chib's throat is closing in on itself. He cannot speak. He kneels down and takes Grandpa's hand. Grandpa has a slight smile on his blue lips. Once and for all, he has eluded Accipiter. In his hand is the latest sheet of his Ms.:

THROUGH BALAKLAVAS OF HATE, THEY CHARGE TOWARDS GOD

For most of my life, I have seen only a truly devout few and a great majority of truly indifferent. But there is a new spirit abroad. So many young men and women have revived, not a love for God, but a violent antipathy towards Him. This excites and restores me. Youths like my grandson and Runic shout blasphemies and so worship Him. If they did

not believe, they would never think about
Him. I now have some confidence in the
future.

TO THE STICKS VIA THE STYX

Dressed in black, Chib and his mother go
down the tube entrance to level 13B. It's lumi-
nous-walled, spacious, and the fare is free.
Chib tells the ticket-fido his destination. Behind the wall, the protein computer, no larger
than a human brain, calculates. A coded ticket
slides out of a slot. Chib takes the ticket, and
they go to the bay, a great incurve, where he
sticks the ticket into a slot. Another ticket
protrudes, and a mechanical voice repeats the
information on the ticket in World and LA
English, in case they can't read.

Gondolas shoot into the bay and decelerate
to a stop. Wheelless, they float in a continu-
ally rebalancing graviton field. Sections of the
bay slide back to make ports for the gondolas.
Passengers step into the cages designated for
them. The cages move forward; their doors
open automatically. The passengers step into
the gondolas. They sit down and wait while
the safety meshmold closes over them. From
the recess of the chassis, transparent plastic
curves rise and meet to form a dome.

Automatically timed, monitored by re-
dundant protein computers for safety, the
gondolas wait until the coast is clear. On re-
ceiving the go-ahead, they move slowly out of
the bay to the tube. They pause while getting
another affirmation, trebly checked in micro-
seconds. Then they move swiftly into the tube.

Whoosh! Whoosh! Other gondolas pass
them. The tube glows yellowly as if filled with
electrified gas. The gondola accelerates rapidly. A few are still passing it, but Chib's
speeds up and soon none can catch up with it.
The round posterior of a gondola ahead is a
glimmering quarry that will not be caught until it slows before mooring at its destined bay.
There are not many gondolas in the tube. Despite a 100-million population, there is little
traffic on the north-south route. Most LA-
ers stay in the self-sufficient walls of their
clutches. There is more traffic on the east-
west tubes, since a small percentage prefer
the public ocean beaches to the municipality
swimming pools.

The vehicle screams southward. After a few
minutes, the tube begins to slope down, and
suddenly it is at a 45-degree angle to the horizontal. They flash by level after level.

Through the transparent walls, Chib
glimpses the people and architecture of other
cities. Level 8, Long Beach, is interesting. Its
homes look like two cut-quartz pie plates, one
on top of another, open end on open end, and
the unit mounted on a column of carved

figures, the exit-entrance ramp a flying buttress.

At level 3A, the tube straightens out. Now the gondola races past establishments the sight of which causes Mama to shut her eyes. Chib squeezes his mother's hand and thinks of the half-brother and cousin who are behind the yellowish plastic. This level contains fifteen percent of the population, the retarded, the incurable insane, the too-ugly, the monstrous, the senile aged. They swarm here, the vacant or twisted faces pressed against the tube wall to watch the pretty cars float by.

"Humanitarian" medical science keeps alive the babies that *should*—by Nature's imperative—have died. Ever since the 20th century, humans with defective genes have been saved from death. Hence, the continual spreading of these genes. The tragic thing is that science can now detect and correct defective genes in the ovum and sperm. Theoretically, all human beings could be blessed with totally healthy bodies and physically perfect brains. But the rub is that we don't have near enough doctors and facilities to keep up with the births. This despite the ever decreasing drop in the birth rate.

Medical science keeps people living so long that senility strikes. So, more and more slobbering mindless decrepits. And also an accelerating addition of the mentally addled. There are therapies and drugs to restore most of

them to "normalcy," but not enough doctors
and facilities. Some day there may be, but
that doesn't help the contemporary unfortu-
nate.

What to do now? The ancient Greeks placed
defective babies in the fields to die. The
Eskimos shipped out their old people on ice
floes. Should we gas our abnormal infants
and seniles? Sometimes, I think it's the merci-
ful thing to do. But I can't ask somebody else
to pull the switch when I won't.

I would shoot the first man to reach for it.
—from Grandpa's *Private Ejaculations*

The gondola approaches one of the rare
intersections. Its passengers see down the
broad-mouthed tube to their right. An express
flies towards them; it looms. Collision course.
They know better, but they can't keep from
gripping the mesh, gritting their teeth, and
bracing their legs. Mama gives a small shriek.
The flier hurtles over them and disappears,
the flapping scream of air a soul on its way to
underworld judgment.

The tube dips again until it levels out on 1.
They see the round below and the massive
self-adjusting pillars supporting the megalopolis. They whiz by over a little town, quaint,
early 21st century LA preserved as a museum,
one of many beneath the cube.

Fifteen minutes after embarking, the Win-
negans reach the end of the line. An eleva-

tor takes them to the ground, where they enter a big black limousine. This is furnished
by a private-enterprise mortuary, since Uncle
Sam or the LA government will pay for crema-
tion but not for burial. The Church no longer
insists on interment, leaving it to the reli-
gionists to choose between being wind-blown
ashes or underground corpses.

The sun is halfway towards the zenith.
Mama begins to have trouble breathing and
her arms and neck redden and swell. The
three times she's been outside the walls, she's
been attacked with this allergy despite the air
conditioning of the limousine. Chib pats her
hand while they're riding over a roughly
patched road. The archaic eighty-year-old,
fuel-cell-powered, electric-motor-driven vehicle is, however, rough-riding only by com-
parison with the gondola. It covers the ten
kilometers to the cemetery speedily, stopping
once to let deer cross the road.

Father Fellini greets them. He is distressed
because he is forced to tell them that the
Church feels that Grandpa has committed
sacrilege. To substitute another man's body
for his corpse, to have mass said over it. to
have it buried in sacred ground is to blaspheme. Moreover, Grandpa died an unre-
pentant criminal. At least, to the knowledge
of the Church, he made no contrition just
before he died.

Chib expects this refusal. St. Mary's of
BH-14 has declined to perform services for

Grandpa within its walls. But Grandpa has often told Chib that he wants to be buried beside his ancestors, and Chib is determined that Grandpa will get his wish.

Chib says, "I'll bury him myself! Right on the edge of the graveyard!"

"You can't do that!" the priest, mortuary officials, and a federal agent say simultaneously.

"The Hell I can't! Where's the shovel?"

It is then that he sees the thin dark face and falciform nose of Accipiter. The agent is supervising the digging up of Grandpa's (first) coffin. Nearby are at least fifty fido men shooting with their minicameras, the transceivers floating a few decameters near them. Grandpa is getting full coverage, as befits the Last Of The Billionaires and The Greatest Criminal Of The Century.

Fido interviewer: "Mr. Accipiter, could we have a few words from you? I'm not exaggerating when I say that there are probably at least ten billion people watching this historic event. After all, even the grade-school kids know of Win-again Winnegan.

"How do you feel about this? You've been on the case for 26 years. The successful conclusion must give you great satisfaction."

Accipiter, unsmiling as the essence of diorite: "Well, actually, I've not devoted full time to this case. Only about three years of accumulative time. But since I've spent at least several days each month on it, you might say I've been on Winnegan's trail for 26 years."

Interviewer: "It's been said that the ending of this case also means the end of the IRB. If we've not been misinformed, the IRB was only kept functioning because of Winnegan. You had other business, of course, during this time, but the tracking down of counterfeiters and gamblers who don't report their income has been turned over to other bureaus. Is this true? If so, what do you plan to do?"

Accipiter, voice flashing a crystal of emotion: "Yes, the IRB is being disbanded. But not until after the case against Winnegan's grand-daughter and her son is finished. They harbored him and are, therefore, accessories after the fact.

"In fact, almost the entire population of Beverly Hills, level 14, should be on trial. I know, but can't prove it as yet, that everybody, including the municipal Chief of Police, was well aware that Winnegan was hiding in that house. Even Winnegan's priest knew it, since Winnegan frequently went to mass and to confession. His priest claims that he urged Winnegan to turn himself in and also refused to give him absolution unless he did so.

"But Winnegan, a hardened 'mouse'—I mean, criminal, if ever I saw one, refused to follow the priest's urgings. He claimed that he had not committed a crime, that, believe it or not, Uncle Sam was the criminal. Imagine the effrontery, the depravity, of the man!"

Interviewer: "Surely you don't plan to arrest the entire population of Beverly Hills 14?"

Accipiter: "I have been advised not to."

Interviewer: "Do you plan on retiring after this case is wound up?"

Accipiter: "No. I intend to transfer to the Greater LA Homicide Bureau. Murder for profit hardly exists any more, but there are still crimes of passion, thank God!"

Interviewer: "Of course, if young Winnegan should win his case against you—he has charged you with invasion of domestic privacy, illegal housebreaking, and directly causing his great-great-grandfather's death—then you won't be able to work for the Homicide Bureau or any police department."

Accipiter, flashing several crystals of emotion: "It's no wonder we law enforcers have such a hard time operating effectively! Sometimes, not only the majority of citizens seem to be on the law-breaker's side but my own employers . . ."

Interviewer: "Would you care to complete that statement? I'm sure your employers are watching this channel. No? I understand that Winnegan's trial and yours are, for some reason, scheduled to take place *at the same time*. How do you plan to be present at both trials? Heh, heh! Some fido-casters are calling you The Simultaneous Man!"

Accipiter, face darkening: "Some idiot clerk did that! He incorrectly fed the data into the legal computer. And he, or somebody, turned off the error-override circuit, and the computer burned up. The clerk is suspected of deliberately making the error—by me anyway, and let the idiot sue me if he wishes—anyway, there have been too many cases like this, and . . ."

Interviewer: "Would you mind summing up the course of this case for our viewers' benefit? Just the highlights, please."

Accipiter: "Well, ah, as you know, fifty years ago all large private-enterprise businesses had become government bureaus. All except the building construction firm, the Finnegan Fifty-three States Company, of which the president was Finn Finnegan. He was the father of the man who is to be buried —somewhere—today.

"Also, all unions except the largest, the construction union, were dissolved or were government unions. Actually, the company and its union were one, because all employees got ninety-five per cent of the money, distributed more or less equally among them. Old Finnegan was both the company president and union business agent-secretary.

"By hook or crook, mainly by crook, I believe, the firm-union had resisted the inevitable absorption. There were investigations into Finnegan's methods: coercion and blackmail of U.S. Senators and even U.S. Supreme Court Justices. Nothing was, however, proved."

Interviewer: "For the benefit of our viewers who may be a little hazy on their history, even fifty years ago money was used only for the purchase of nonguaranteed items. Its other use, as today, was as an index of prestige and social esteem. At one time, the government was thinking of getting rid of currency entirely, but a study revealed that it had great psychological value. The income tax was also kept, although the government had no use for money, because the size of a man's tax determined prestige and also because it enabled the government to remove a large amount of currency from circulation."

Accipiter: "Anyway, when old Finnegan died, the federal government renewed its pressure to incorporate the construction workers and the company officials as civil servants. But young Finnegan proved to be as foxy and vicious as his old man. I don't suggest, of course, that the fact that his uncle was President of the U.S. at that time had anything to do with young Finnegan's success."

Interviewer: "Young Finnegan was seventy years old when his father died."

Accipiter: "During this struggle, which went on for many years, Finnegan decided to rename himself Winnegan. It's a pun on Win Again. He seems to have had a childish, even imbecilic, delight in puns, which, frankly, I don't understand. Puns, I mean."

Interviewer: "For the benefit of our non-American viewers, who may not know of our national custom of Naming Day . . . this was originated by the Panamorites. When a citizen comes of age, he may at any time thereafter take a new name, one which he believes to be appropriate to his temperament or goal in life. I might point out that Uncle Sam, who's been unfairly accused of trying to impose conformity upon his citizens, encourages this individualistic approach to life. This despite the increased record-keeping required on the government's part.

"I might also point out something else of interest. The government claimed that Grandpa Winnegan was mentally incompetent. My listeners will pardon me, I hope, if I take up a moment of your time to explain the basis of Uncle Sam's assertion. Now, for the benefit of those among you who are unacquainted with an early 20th-century classic, *Finnegan's Wake*, despite your government's wish for you to have a free lifelong education, the author, James Joyce, derived the title from an old vaudeville song."

(Half-fadeout while a monitor briefly explains "vaudeville.")

"The song was about Tim Finnegan, an Irish hod carrier who fell off a ladder while drunk and was supposedly killed. During the Irish wake held for Finnegan, the corpse is accidentally splashed with whiskey. Finnegan, feeling the touch of the whiskey, the 'water of life,' sits up in his coffin and then climbs out to drink and dance with the mourners.

"Grandpa Winnegan always claimed that the vaudeville song was based on reality, you can't keep a good man down, and that the original Tim Finnegan was his ancestor. This preposterous statement was used by the government in its suit against Winnegan.

"However, Winnegan produced documents to substantiate his assertion. Later—too late—the documents were proved to be forgeries."

Accipiter: "The government's case against Winnegan was strengthened by the rank and file's sympathy with the government. Citizens were complaining that the business-union was undemocratic and discriminatory. The officials and workers were getting relatively high wages, but many citizens had to be contented with their guaranteed income. So, Winnegan was brought to trial and accused, justly, of course, of various crimes, among which were subversion of democracy.

"Seeing the inevitable, Winnegan capped his criminal career. He somehow managed to steal 20 billion dollars from the federal deposit vault. This sum, by the way, was equal to half the currency then existing in Greater LA. Winnegan disappeared with the money, which he had not only stolen but had not paid income tax on. Unforgivable. I don't know why so many people have glamorized this villain's feat. Why, I've even seen fido shows with him as the hero, thinly disguised under another name, of course."

Interviewer: "Yes, folks, Winnegan committed the Crime Of The Age. And, although he has finally been located, and is to be buried today—somewhere—the case is not completely closed. The federal government says it is. But where is the money, the 20 billion dollars?"

Accipiter: "Actually, the money has no value now except as collector's items. Shortly after the theft, the government called in all currency and then issued new bills that could not be mistaken for the old. The government had been wanting to do something like this for a long time, anyway, because it believed that there was too much currency, and it only reissued half the amount taken in.

"I'd like very much to know where the money is. I won't rest until I do. I'll hunt it down if I have to do it on my own time."

Interviewer: "You may have plenty of time to do that if young Winnegan wins his case. Well, folks, as most of you may know, Winnegan was found dead in a lower level of San Francisco about a year after he disappeared. His grand-daughter identified the body, and the fingerprints, earprints, retinaprints, teethprints, blood-type, hair-type, and a dozen other identity prints matched out."

Chib, who has been listening, thinks that Grandpa must have spent several millions of the stolen money arranging this. He does not know, but he suspects that a research lab somewhere in the world grew the duplicate in a biotank.

This happened two years after Chib was born. When Chib was five, his grandpa showed up. Without letting Mama know he was back, he moved in. Only Chib was his confidant. It was, of course, impossible for Grandpa to go completely unnoticed by Mama, yet she now insisted that she had never seen him. Chib thought that this was to avoid prosecution for being an accessory after the crime. He was not sure. Perhaps she had blocked off his "visitations" from the rest of her mind. For her it would be easy, since she never knew whether today was Tuesday or Thursday and could not tell you what year it was.

Chib ignores the mortuarians, who want to know what to do with the body. He walks over to the grave. The top of the ovoid coffin is visible now, with the long elephantlike snout of the digging machine sonically crumbling the dirt and then sucking it up. Accipiter, breaking through his lifelong control, is smiling at the fidomen and rubbing his hands.

"Dance a little, you son of a bitch," Chib says, his anger the only block to the tears and wail building up in him.

The area around the coffin is cleared to make room for the grappling arms of the machine. These descend, hook under, and lift the black, irradiated-plastic, mocksilver-arabesqued coffin up and out onto the grass.

Chib, seeing the IRB men begin to open the coffin, starts to say something but closes his mouth. He watches intently, his knees bent as if getting ready to jump. The fidomen close in, their eyeball-shaped cameras pointing at the group around the coffin.

Groaning, the lid rises. There is a big bang. Dense dark smoke billows. Accipiter and his men, blackened, eyes wide and white, coughing, stagger out of the cloud. The fidomen are running every which way or stooping to pick up their cameras. Those who were standing far enough back can see that the explosion took place at the bottom of the grave. Only Chib knows that the raising of the coffin lid has activated the detonating device in the grave.

He is also the first to look up into the sky at the projectile soaring from the grave because only he expected it. The rocket climbs up to five hundred feet while the fidomen train their cameras on it. It bursts apart and from it a ribbon unfolds between two round objects. The objects expand to become balloons while the ribbon becomes a huge banner.

On it, in big black letters, are the words

WINNEGAN'S FAKE!

Twenty billions of dollars buried beneath the supposed bottom of the grave burn furiously. Some bills, blown up in the geyser of fireworks, are carried by the wind while IRB men, fidomen, mortuary officials, and municipality officials chase them.

Mama is stunned.

Accipiter looks as if he is having a stroke.

Chib cries and then laughs and rolls on the ground.

Grandpa has again screwed Uncle Sam and has also pulled his greatest pun where all the world can see it.

"Oh, you old man!" Chib sobs between laughing fits. "Oh, you old man! How I love you!"

While he is rolling on the ground again, roaring so hard his ribs hurt, he feels a paper in his hand. He stops and gets on his knees and calls after the man who gave it to him. The man says, "I was paid by your grandfather to hand it to you when he was buried."

Chib reads.

I hope nobody was hurt, not even the IRB men.

Final advice from the Wise Old Man In The Cave. Tear loose. Leave LA. Leave the country. Go to Egypt. Let your mother ride the purple wage on her own. She can do it if she practices thrift and self-denial. If she can't, that's not your fault.

You are fortunate indeed to have been born with talent, if not genius, and to be strong enough to want to rip out the umbilical cord. So do it. Go to Egypt. Steep yourself in the ancient culture. Stand before the Sphinx. Ask her (actually, it's a he) the Question.

Then visit one of the zoological preserves south of the Nile. Live for a while in a reasonable facsimile of Nature as she was before mankind dishonored and disfigured her. There, where Homo Sapiens (?) evolved from the killer ape, absorb the spirit of that ancient place and time.

You've been painting with your penis, which I'm afraid was more stiffened with bile than with passion for life. Learn to paint with your heart. Only thus will you become great and true.

Paint.

Then, go wherever you want to go. I'll be with you as long as you're alive to remember me. To quote Runic, "I'll be the Northern Lights of your soul."

Hold fast to the belief that there will be others to love you just as much as I did or even more. What is more important, you must love them as much as they love you.

Can you do this?

II

SPIDERS OF THE
PURPLE MAGE

This was the week of the great rat hunt in Sanctuary.

The next week, all the cats that could be caught were killed and degutted.

The third week, all dogs were run down and disemboweled.

Masha zil-Ineel was one of the very few people in the city who didn't take part in the rat hunt. She just couldn't believe that any rat, no matter how big, and there were some huge ones in Sanctuary, could swallow a jewel so large.

But when a rumor spread that someone had seen a cat eat a dead rat and that the cat had acted strangely afterward, she thought it wise to pretend to chase cats. If she hadn't, people might wonder why not. They might think that she knew something they didn't. And then she might be the one run down.

Unlike the animals, however, she'd be tortured until she told where the jewel was.

She didn't know where it was. She wasn't even sure that there *was* an emerald.

But everybody knew that she'd been told about the jewel by Benna nus-Katarz. Thanks to Masha's blabbermouth drunken husband, Eevroen.

Three weeks ago, on a dark night, Masha had returned late from midwifing in the rich merchant's eastern quarter. It was well past midnight, but she wasn't sure of the hour because of the cloud-covered sky. The second wife of Shoozh the spice-importer had borne her fourth infant. Masha had attended to the delivery personally while Doctor Nadeesh had sat in the next room, the door only half-closed, and listened to her reports. Nadeesh was forbidden to see any part of a female client except for those normally exposed and especially forbidden to see the breasts and genitals. If there was any trouble with the birthing, Masha would inform him, and he would give her instructions.

This angered Masha, since the doctors collected half of the fee, yet were seldom of any use. In fact, they were usually a hindrance.

Still, half a fee was better than none. What if the wives and concubines of the wealthy

were as nonchalant and hardy as the poor
women, who just squatted down wherever
they happened to be when the pangs started
and gave birth unassisted? Masha could not
have supported herself, her two daughters,
her invalid mother, or her lazy alcoholic husband. The money she made from doing the
more affluent women's hair and from her
tooth-pulling and manufacture of false teeth
in the marketplace wasn't enough. But mid-
wifery added the income that kept her and her
family just outside hunger's door.

She would have liked to pick up more
money by cutting men's hair in the marketplace, but both law and ancient custom for-
bade that.

Shortly after she had burned the umbilical
cord of the newborn to ensure that demons
didn't steal it and had ritualistically washed
her hands, she left Shoozh's house. His
guards, knowing her, let her through the gate
without challenge, and the guards of the gate
to the eastern quarters also allowed her to
pass. Not however without offers from a few
to share their beds with her that night.

"I can do much better than that sot of a husband of yours!" one said.

Masha was glad that her hood and the darkness prevented the guards from seeing her
burning face by the torchlight. However, if
they could have seen that she was blushing
with shame, they might have been embarrassed. They would know then that they

weren't dealing with a brazen slut of the Maze
but with a woman who had known better days
and a higher position in society than she now
held. The blush alone would have told them
that.

What they didn't know and what she
couldn't forget was that she had once lived in
this walled area and her father had been an
affluent, if not wealthy, merchant.

She passed on silently. It would have made
her feel good to have told them her past and
then ripped them with the invective she'd
learned in the Maze. But to do that would
lower her estimate of herself.

Though she had her own torch and the
means for lighting it in the cylindrical leather
case on her back, she did not use them. It was
better to walk unlit and hence unseen into the
streets. Though many of the lurkers in the
shadows would let her pass unmolested, since
they had known her when she was a child,
others would not be so kind. They would rob
her for the tools of her trade and the clothes
she wore and some would rape her. Or try to.

Through the darkness she went swiftly, her
steps sure because of long experience. The
adobe buildings of the city were a dim whitish
bulk ahead. Then the path took a turn, and she
saw some small flickers of light here and
there. Torches. A little further, and a light became a square. The window of a tavern.

She entered a narrow winding street and
strode down its center. Turning a corner, she

saw a torch in a bracket on the wall of a house and two men standing near it. Immediately she crossed to the far side and, hugging the walls, passed the two. Their pipes glowed redly; she caught a whiff of the pungent and sickly smoke of *kleetel*, the drug used by the poor when they didn't have money for the more expensive *krrf*. Which was most of the time.

After two or three pipefuls, the smokers would be vomiting. But they would claim that the euphoria would make the upchucking worth it.

There were other odors: garbage piled by the walls, slop-jars of excrement, and puke from *kleetel* smokers and drunks. The garbage would be shoveled into goat-drawn carts by Downwinders whose families had long held this right. The slop-jars would be emptied by a Downwinder family that had delivered the contents to farmers for a century and would and had fought fiercely to keep this right. The farmers would use the excrement to feed their soil; the urine would be emptied into the mouth of the White Foal River and carried out to sea.

She also heard the rustling and squealing of rats as they searched for edible portions and dogs growling or snarling as they chased the rats or fought each other. And she glimpsed the swift shadows of running cats.

Like a cat, she sped down the street in a half-run, stopping at corners to look around them before venturing farther. When she was about a half-mile from her place, she heard the pounding of feet ahead. She froze and tried to make herself look like part of the wall.

At that moment the moon broke through the clouds.

It was almost a full moon. The light revealed her to any but a blind person. She darted across the street to the dark side and played wall again.

The slap of feet on the hard-packed dirt of the street came closer. Somewhere above her, a baby began crying.

She pulled a long knife from a scabbard under her cloak and held the blade behind her. Doubtless, the one running was a thief or else someone trying to outrun a thief or mugger or muggers or perhaps a throat-slitter. If it was a thief who was getting away from the site of the crime, she would be safe. He'd be in no position to stop to see what he could get from her. If he was being pursued, the pursuers might shift their attention to her.

If they saw her.

Suddenly, the pound of feet became louder. Around the corner came a tall youth dressed in a ragged tunic and breeches and shod with buskins. He stopped and clutched the corner and looked behind him. His breath rasped like a rusty gate swung back and forth by gusts of wind.

Somebody was after him. Should she wait here? He hadn't seen her, and perhaps whoever was chasing him would be so intent he or they wouldn't detect her either.

The youth turned his face, and she gasped. His face was so swollen that she almost didn't recognize him. But he was Benna nus-Katarz, who had come here from Ilsig two years ago. No one knew why he'd immigrated, and no one, in keeping with the unwritten code of Sanctuary, had asked him why.

Even in the moonlight and across the street, she could see the swellings and dark spots, looking like bruises, on his face. And on his hands. The fingers were rotting bananas.

He turned back to peer around the corner. His breathing became less heavy. Now she could hear the faint slap of feet down the street. His chasers would be here soon.

Benna gave a soft ululation of despair. He staggered down the street toward a mound of garbage and stopped before it. A rat scuttled out but stopped a few feet from him and chittered at him. Bold beasts, the rats of Sanctuary.

Now Masha could hear the loudness of approaching runners and words that sounded like sheets being ripped apart.

Benna moaned. He reached under his tunic

with clumsy fingers and drew something out.
Masha couldn't see what it was, though she
strained. She inched with her back to the wall
toward a doorway. Its darkness would make
her even more undetectable.

Benna looked at the thing in his hand. He
said something which sounded to Masha like
a curse. She couldn't be sure; he spoke in the
Ilsig dialect.

The baby above had ceased crying; its
mother must have given it the nipple or perhaps she'd made it drink water tinctured with
a drug.

Now Benna was pulling something else
from inside his tunic. Whatever it was, he
molded it around the other thing, and now he
had cast it in front of the rat.

The big gray beast ran away as the object
arced toward him. A moment later, it approached the little ball, sniffing. Then it
darted forward, still smelling it, touched it
with its nose, perhaps tasted it, and was gone
with it in its mouth.

Masha watched it squeeze into a crack in
the old adobe building at the next corner. No
one lived there. It had been crumbling, falling
down for years, unrepaired and avoided even
by the most desperate of transients and bums.
It was said that the ghost of old Lahboo the
Tight-Fisted haunted the place since his
murder, and no one cared to test the truth of
the stories told about the building.

Benna, still breathing somewhat heavily,

trotted after the rat. Masha, hearing that the footsteps were louder, went alongside the wall, still in the shadows. She was curious about what Benna had gotten rid of, but she didn't want to be associated with him in any way when his hunters caught up with him.

At the corner, the youth stopped and looked around him. He didn't seem able to make up his mind which route to take. He stood, swaying, and then fell to his knees. He groaned and pitched forward, softening his fall with outstretched arms.

Masha meant to leave him to his fate. It was the only sensible thing to do. But as she rounded the corner, she heard him moaning. And then she thought she heard him say something about a jewel.

She stopped. Was that what he had put in something, perhaps a bit of cheese, and thrown to the rat? It would be worth more money than she'd earn in a lifetime, and if she could, somehow, get her hands on it . . . Her thoughts raced as swiftly as her heart, and now she was breathing heavily. A jewel! A jewel? It would mean release from this terrible place, a good home for her mother and her children. And for herself.

And it might mean release from Eevroen.

But there was also a terrible danger very close. She couldn't hear the sounds of the pursuers now, but that didn't mean they'd left the neighborhood. They were prowling around, looking into each doorway. Or perhaps one

had looked around the corner and seen
Benna. He had motioned to the others, and
they were just behind the corner, getting
ready to make a sudden rush.

She could visualize the knives in their
hands.

If she took a chance and lost, she'd die, and
her mother and daughters would be without
support. They'd have to beg; Eevroen certainly would be of no help. And Handoo and
Kheem, three and five years old, would grow
up, if they didn't die first, to be child whores.
It was almost inevitable.

While she stood undecided, knowing that
she had only a few seconds to act and perhaps
not that, the clouds slid below the moon
again. That made the difference in what she'd
do. She ran across the street toward Benna.
He was still lying in the dirt of the street, his
head only a few inches from some stinking
dog turds. She scabbarded her dagger, got
down on her knees, and rolled him over. He
gasped with terror when he felt her hands
upon him.

"It's all right!" she said softly. "Listen!
Can you get up if I help you? I'll get you
away!"

Sweat poured into her eyes as she looked
toward the far corner. She could see nothing,
but if the hunters wore black, they wouldn't
be visible at this distance.

Benna moaned and then said, "I'm dying,
Masha."

Masha gritted her teeth. She had hoped that he'd not recognize her voice, not at least until she'd gotten him to safety. Now, if the hunters found him alive and got her name from him, they'd come after her. They'd think she had the jewel or whatever it was they wanted.

"Here. Get up," she said, and struggled to help him. She was small, about five feet tall and weighing eighty-two pounds. But she had the muscles of a cat, and fear was pumping strength into her. She managed to get Benna to his feet. Staggering under his weight, she supported him toward the open doorway of the building on the corner.

Benna reeked of something strange, an odor of rotting meat but unlike any she'd ever smelled. It rode over the stale sweat and urine of his body and clothes.

"No use," Benna mumbled through greatly swollen lips. "I'm dying. The pain is terrible, Masha."

"Keep going!" she said fiercely. "We're almost there!"

Benna raised his head. His eyes were surrounded with puffed-out flesh. Masha had never seen such edema; the blackness and the swelling looked like those of a corpse five days dead in the heat of summer.

"No!" he mumbled. "Not old Lahboo's building!"

Under other circumstances, Masha would have laughed. Here was a dying man or a man who thought he was dying. And he'd be dead soon if his pursuers caught up with him. (Me, too, she thought.) Yet he was afraid to take the only refuge available because of a ghost.

"You look bad enough to scare even The Tight-Fisted One," she said. "Keep going or I'll drop you right now!"

She got him inside the doorway, though it wasn't easy what with the boards still attached to the lower half of the entrance. The top planks had fallen inside. It was a tribute to the fear people felt for this place that no one had stolen the wood, an expensive item in the desert town.

Just after they'd climbed over, Benna almost falling, she heard a man utter something in a raspy tearing language. He was nearby, but he must have just arrived. Otherwise, he would have heard the two.

Masha had thought she'd reached the limits of terror, but she found that she hadn't. The speaker was a Raggah!

Though she couldn't understand the speech —no one in Sanctuary could—she'd heard Raggah a number of times. Every thirty days or so five or six of the cloaked, robed, hooded, and veiled desert men came to the bazaar and the farmers' market. They could speak only their own language, but they used signs and a plentitude of coins to obtain what they wanted. Then they departed on their horses, their mules loaded down with food, wine, *vuksibah* (the very expensive malt whiskey imported from a far north land), goods of various kinds: clothing, bowls, braziers, ropes, camel and horse hides. Their camels bore huge panniers full of feed for chickens, ducks, camels, horses, and hogs. They also purchased steel tools: shovels, picks, drills, hammers, wedges.

They were tall, and though they were very dark, most had blue or green eyes. These looked cold and hard and piercing, and few looked directly into them. It was said that they had the gift, or the curse, of the evil eye.

They were enough, in this dark night, to have made Masha marble with terror. But what was worse, and this galvanized the marble, they were the servants of the purple mage!

Masha guessed at once what had happened. Benna had had the guts—and the complete stupidity—to sneak into the underground maze of the mage on the river isle of Shugthee and to steal a jewel. It was amazing that he'd had the courage, astounding that he could get undetected into the caves, an absolute wonder that he'd penetrated the treasurehold, and fantastic that he'd managed to get out. What weird tales he could tell if he survived! Masha

could think of no similar event, no analog, to
the adventures he must have had.

"Mofandsf!" she thought. In the thieves'
argot of Sanctuary, "Mind-boggling!"

At that moment Benna's knees gave, and it
was all she could do to hold him up. Somehow, she got him to the door to the next room
and into a closet. If the Raggah came in, they
would look here, of course, but she could get
him no further.

Benna's odor was even more sickening in
the hot confines of the closet, though its door
was almost completely open. She eased him
down. He mumbled, "Spiders . . . spiders."

She put her mouth close to his ear. "Don't
talk loudly, Benna. The Raggah are close by.
Benna, what did you say about the spiders?"

"Bites . . . bites," he murmured. "Hurt . . .
the . . . the emerald . . . rich . . . !"

"How'd you get in?" she said. She put her
hand close to his mouth to clamp down on it if
he should start to talk loudly.

"Wha . . . ? Camel's eye . . . bu . . . "

He stiffened, the heels of his feet striking
the bottom of the closet door. Masha pressed
her hand down on his mouth. She was afraid
that he might cry out in his death agony. If
this were it. And it was. He groaned, and then
relaxed. Masha took her hand away. A long
sigh came from his open mouth.

She looked around the edge of the closet.
Though it was dark outside, it was brighter
than the darkness in the house. She should be

able to make out anyone standing in the doorway. The noise the heels made could have attracted the hunters. She saw no one, though it was possible that someone had already come in and was against a wall. Listening for more noise.

She felt Benna's pulse. He was dead or so close to it that it didn't matter any more. She rose and slowly pulled her dagger from the scabbard. Then she stepped out, crouching, sure that the thudding of her heart could be heard in this still room.

So unexpectedly and suddenly that a soft cry was forced from her, a whistle sounded outside. Feet pounded in the room—there *was* someone here!—and the dim rectangle of the doorway showed a bulk plunging through it. But it was going out, not in. The Raggah had heard the whistle of the garrison soldiers— half the city must have heard it—and he was leaving with his fellows.

She turned and bent down and searched under Benna's tunic and in his loincloth. She found nothing except slowly cooling lumpy flesh. Within ten seconds, she was out on the street. Down a block was the advancing light of torches, their holders not yet visible. In the din of shouts and whistles, she fled hoping that she wouldn't run into any laggard Raggah or another body of soldiers.

Later, she found out that she'd been saved because the soldiers were looking for a prisoner who'd escaped from the dungeon.

His name was Badniss, but that's another
tale.

Masha's two-room apartment was on the
third floor of a large adobe building which,
with two others, occupied an entire block. She
entered it on the side of the Street of the Dry
Well, but first she had to wake up old Shmurt,
the caretaker, by beating on the thick oaken
door. Grumbling at the late hour, he unshot
the bolt and let her in. She gave him a *pad-
pool*, a tiny copper coin, for his trouble and to
shut him up. He handed her her oil lamp, she
lit it, and she went up the three flights of stone
steps.

She had to wake up her mother to get in.
Wallu, blinking and yawning in the light of an
oil lamp in the corner, shot the bolt. Masha
entered and at once extinguished her lamp.
Oil cost money, and there had been many
nights when she had had to do without it.

Wallu, a tall skinny sagging-breasted woman of fifty, with gaunt deeply-lined features,
kissed her daughter on the cheek. Her breath
was sour with sleep and goat's cheese. But
Masha appreciated the peck; her life had little
expressions of love in it. And yet she was full
of it; she was a bottle close to bursting with
pressure.

The light on the rickety table in the corner showed a blank-walled room without rugs. In a far corner the two infants slept on a pile of tattered but clean blankets. Beside them was a small chamberpot of baked clay painted with the black and scarlet rings-within-rings of the Darmek guild.

In another corner was her false-teeth making equipment, wax, molds, tiny chisels, saws, and expensive wire, hardwood, iron, a block of ivory. She had only recently repaid the money she'd borrowed to purchase these. In the opposite corner was another pile of cloth, Wallu's bed, and beside it another thundermug with the same design. An ancient and wobbly spinning wheel was near it; Wallu made some money with it, though not much. Her hands were gnarled with arthritis, one eye had a cataract, and the other was beginning to lose its sight for some unknown reason.

Along the adobe wall was a brass charcoal brazier and above it a wooden vent. A bin held charcoal. A big cabinet beside it held grain and some dried meat and plates and knives. Near it was a baked clay vase for water. Next to it was a pile of cloths.

Wallu pointed at the curtain in the doorway to the other room.

"He came home early. I suppose he couldn't cadge drinks enough from his friends. But he's drunk enough to suit a dozen sailors."

Grimacing, Masha strode to the curtain and

pulled it aside.

"Shewaw!" (A combination of "Whew!",
"Ugh!", and "Yech!")

The stink was that which greeted her nostrils when she opened the door to The Vulgar
Unicorn Tavern. A blend of wine and beer,
stale and fresh, sweat, stale and fresh, vomit,
urine, frying blood-sausages, *krrf,* and *kleetel.*

Eevroen lay on his back, his mouth open,
his arms spread out as if he were being cruci-
fied. Once, he had been a tall muscular youth,
very broad-shouldered, slim-waisted, and
long-legged. Now he was fat, fat, fat, double-
chinned, huge-paunched with rings of sagging
fat around his waist. The once-bright eyes
were red and dark-bagged, and the once-sweet
breath was a hellpit of stenches. He'd fallen
asleep without changing into nightclothes; his
tunic was ripped, dirty, and stained with
various things, including puke. He wore cast-
off sandals, or perhaps he'd stolen them.

Masha was long past weeping over him. She
kicked him in the ribs, causing him to grunt
and to open one eye. But it closed and he was
quickly snoring like a pig again. That, at least,
was a blessing. How many nights had she
spent in screaming at him while he bellowed
at her or in fighting him off when he staggered home and insisted she lie with him? She
didn't want to count them.

Masha would have gotten rid of him long
ago if she had been able to. But the law of the
empire was that only the man could divorce

unless the woman could prove her spouse was too diseased to have children or was impotent.

She whirled and walked toward the wash basin. As she passed her mother, a hand stopped her.

Wallu, peering at her with one half-good eye, said, "Child! Something has happened to you! What was it?"

"Tell you in a moment," Masha said, and she washed her face and hands and armpits. Later, she regretted very much that she hadn't told Wallu a lie. But how was she to know that Eevroen had come out of his stupor enough to hear what she said? If only she hadn't been so furious that she'd kicked him . . . but regrets were a waste of time, though there wasn't a human alive who didn't indulge in them.

She had no sooner finished telling her mother what had happened with Benna when she heard a grunt behind her. She turned to see Eevroen swaying in front of the curtains, a stupid grin on his fat face. The face once so beloved.

Eevroen reeled toward her, his hands out as if he intended to grab her. He spoke thickly but intelligibly enough.

"Why'n't you go affer the rat? If you caught it, we coulda been rich?"

"Go back to sleep," Masha said. "This has nothing to do with you."

"Nothin' do wi' me?" Eevroen bellowed. "Wha' you mean? I'm your husband! Wha'ss yoursh ish mine. I wan' tha' jewel!''

"You damned fool," Masha said, trying to keep from screaming so that the children wouldn't wake and the neighbors wouldn't hear, "I don't have the jewel. There was no way I could get it—if there ever was any."

Eevroen put a finger alongside his nose and winked the left eye. "If there wa' ever any, heh? Masha, you tryna hol' ou' on me? You go' the jewel, and you lyin' to you' mo . . . mo . . . mama."

"No, I'm not lying!" she screamed, all reason for caution having deserted her quite unreasonably. "You fat stinking pig! I've had a terrible time, I almost got killed, and all you can think about is the jewel! Which probably doesn't exist! Benna was dying! He didn't know what he was talking about! I never saw the jewel! And . . ."

Eevroen snarled, "You tryna keep i' from me!" and he charged her.

She could easily have evaded him, but something swelled up in her and took over, and she seized a baked-clay water jug from a shelf and brought it down hard over his head. The jug didn't break, but Eevroen did. He fell face forward. Blood welled from his scalp; he snored.

By then the children were awake, sitting up, wide-eyed, but silent. Maze children learned at an early age not to cry easily.

Shaking, Masha got down on her knees and examined the wound. Then she rose and went to the rag rack and returned with some dirty ones, no use wasting clean ones on him, and stanched the wound. She felt his pulse; it was beating steadily enough for a drunkard who'd just been knocked out with a severe blow.

Wallu said, "Is he dead?"

She wasn't concerned about him. She was worrying about herself, the children, and Masha. If her daughter should be executed for killing her husband, however justified she was, then she and the girls would be without support.

"He'll have a hell of a headache in the morning," Masha said. With some difficulty, she rolled Eevroen over so that he would be face down, and she turned his head sideways and then put some rags under the side of his head. Now, if he should vomit during the night, he wouldn't choke to death. For a moment she was tempted to put him back as he had fallen. But the judge might think that she was responsible for his death.

"Let him lie there," she said. "I'm not going to break my back dragging him to our bed. Besides, I wouldn't be able to sleep, he snores so loudly and he stinks so badly."

She should have been frightened of what he'd do in the morning. But, strangely, she felt exuberant. She'd done what she'd wanted to do for several years now, and the deed had discharged much of her anger—for the time being, anyway.

She went to her room and tossed and turned

for a while, thinking of how much better life would be if she could get rid of Eevroen.

Her last thoughts were of what life could be if she'd gotten the jewel that Benna had thrown to the rat.

She awoke an hour or so past dawn, a very late time for her, and smelled bread baking. After she'd sat on the chamberpot, she rose and pushed the curtain aside. She was curious about the lack of noise in the next room. Eevroen was gone. So were the children. Wallu, hearing the little bells on the curtain, turned.

"I sent the children out to play," she said. "Eevroen woke up about dawn. He pretended he didn't know what had happened, but I could tell that he did. He groaned now and then—his head I suppose. He ate some breakfast, and then he got out fast."

Wallu smiled. "I think he's afraid of you."

"Good!" Masha said. "I hope he keeps on being afraid."

She sat down while Wallu, hobbling around, served her a half loaf of bread, a hunk of goat cheese, and an orange. Masha wondered if her husband also remembered what she'd said to her mother about Benna and the jewel.

He had.

When she went to the bazaar, carrying the folding chair in which she put her dental patients, she was immediately surrounded by hundreds of men and women. All wanted to know about the jewel.

Masha thought, "The damn fool!"

Eevroen, it seemed, had procured free drinks with his tale. He'd staggered around everywhere, the taverns, the bazaar, the farmers' market, the waterfront, and he'd spread the news. Apparently, he didn't say anything about Masha's knocking him out. That tale would have earned him only derision, and he still had enough manhood left not to reveal that.

At first, Masha was going to deny the story. But it seemed to her that most people would think she was lying, and they would be sure that she had kept the jewel. Her life would be miserable from then on. Or ended. There were plenty who wouldn't hesitate to drag her off to some secluded place and torture her until she told where the jewel was.

So she described exactly what had happened, omitting how she had tried to brain Eevroen. There was no sense in pushing him too hard. If he was humiliated publicly, he might get desperate enough to try to beat her up.

She got only one patient that day. As fast as those who'd heard her tale ran off to look for rats, others took their place. And then, inevitably, the governor's soldiers came. She was surprised they hadn't appeared sooner. Surely one of their informants had sped to the palace as soon as he had heard her story, and that would have been shortly after she'd come to the bazaar.

The sergeant of the soldiers questioned her first, and then she was marched to the garrison, where a captain interrogated her. Afterward, a colonel came in, and she had to repeat her tale. And then, after sitting in a room for at least two hours, she was taken to the governor himself. The handsome youth, surprisingly, didn't detain her long. He seemed to have checked out her movements, starting with Doctor Nadeesh. He'd worked out a timetable between the moment she left Shoozh's house and the moment she came home. So, her mother had also been questioned.

A soldier had seen two of the Raggah running away; their presence was verified.

"Well, Masha," the governor said. "You've stirred up a rat's nest," and he smiled at his own joke while the soldiers and courtiers laughed.

"There is no evidence that there was any jewel," he said, "aside from the story this Benna told, and he was dying from venom and in great pain. My doctor has examined his body, and he assures me that the swellings were spider bites. Of course, he doesn't know everything. He's been wrong before.

"But people are going to believe that there

was indeed a jewel of great value, and nothing anyone says, including myself, will convince them otherwise.

"However, all their frantic activity will result in one great benefit. We'll be rid of the rats for a while."

He paused, frowning, then said, "It would seem, however, that this fellow Benna might have been foolish enough to steal something from the purple mage. I would think that that is the only reason he'd be pursued by the Raggah. But then there might be another reason. In any event, if there is a jewel, then the finder is going to be in great peril. The mage isn't going to let whoever finds it keep it.

"Or at least I believe so. Actually, I know very little about the mage, and from what I've heard about him, I have no desire to meet him."

Masha thought of asking him why he didn't send his soldiers out to the isle and summon the mage. But she kept silent. The reason was obvious. No one, not even the governor, wanted to provoke the wrath of a mage. And as long as the mage did nothing to force the governor into action, he would be left strictly alone to conduct his business—whatever that was.

At the end of the questioning, the governor told his treasurer to give a gold *shaboozh* to Masha.

"That should more than take care of any

business you've lost by being here," the governor said.

Thanking him profusely, Masha bowed as she stepped back, and then walked swiftly homeward.

The following week was the great cat hunt. It was also featured, for Masha anyway, by a break-in into her apartment. While she was off helping deliver a baby at the home of the merchant Ahloo shik-Mhanukhee, three masked men knocked old Shmurt the doorkeeper out and broke down the door to her rooms. While the girls and her mother cowered in a corner, the three ransacked the place, even emptying the chamberpots on the floor to determine that nothing was hidden there.

They didn't find what they were looking for, and one of the frustrated interlopers knocked out two of Wallu's teeth in a rage. Masha was thankful, however, that they did not beat or rape the little girls. That may have been not so much because of their mercifulness as that the doorkeeper regained consciousness sooner than they had expected. He began yelling for help, and the three thugs ran away before the neighbors could gather or the soldiers come.

Eevroen continued to come in drunk late at night. But he spoke very little, just using the place to eat and sleep. He seldom saw Masha when she was awake. In fact, he seemed to be doing his best to avoid her. That was fine with her.

Several times, both by day and night, Masha felt someone was following her. She did her best to detect the shadower, but whether she got the feeling by day or night, she failed to do it. She decided that her nervous state was responsible.

Then the great dog hunt began. Masha thought this was the apex of hysteria and silliness. But it worried her. After all the poor dogs were gone, what would next be run down and killed and gutted? To be more precise, who? She hoped that the who wouldn't be she.

In the middle of the week of the dog hunt, little Kheem became sick. Masha had to go to work, but when she came home after sundown, she found that Kheem was suffering from a high fever. According to her mother, Kheem had also had convulsions. Alarmed, Masha set out at once for Doctor Nadeesh's house in the Eastern quarter. He admitted her and listened to her describe Kheem's symptoms. But he refused to accompany her to her house.

"It's too dangerous to go into the Maze at night," he said. "And I wouldn't go there in the day unless I had several bodyguards. Besides, I am having company tonight. You should have brought the child here."

"She's too sick to be moved," Masha said. "I beg you to come."

Nadeesh was adamant, but he did give her some powders which she could use to cool the child's fever.

She thanked him audibly and cursed him silently. On the way back, while only a block from her apartment, she heard a sudden thud of footsteps behind her. She jumped to one side and whirled, drawing her dagger at the same time. There was no moon, and the nearest light was from oil lamps shining through some iron-barred windows in the second story above her.

By its faintness she saw a dark bulk. It was robed and hooded, a man by its tallness. Then she heard a low hoarse curse and knew it was a man. He had thought to grab or strike her from behind, but Masha's unexpected leap had saved her. Momentarily, at least. Now the man rushed her, and she glimpsed something long and dark in his uplifted hand. A club.

Instead of standing there frozen with fear or trying to run away, she crouched low and charged him. That took him by surprise. Before he could recover, he was struck in the throat with her blade.

Still, his body knocked her down, and he fell hard upon her. For a moment, the breath was knocked out of her. She was helpless, and when another bulk loomed above her, she knew that she had no chance.

The second man, also robed and hooded,

lifted a club to bring it down on her exposed head.

Writhing, pinned down by the corpse, Masha could do nothing but await the blow. She thought briefly of little Kheem, and then she saw the man drop the club. And he was down on his knees, still gripping whatever it was that had closed off his breath.

A moment later, he was face down in the dry dirt, dead or unconscious.

The man standing over the second attacker was short and broad and also robed and hooded. He put something in his pocket, probably the cord he'd used to strangle her attacker, and he approached her cautiously. His hands seemed to be empty, however.

"Masha?" he said softly.

By then she'd recovered her wind. She wriggled out from under the dead man, jerked the dagger from the windpipe, and started to get up.

The man said, in a foreign accent, "You can put your knife away, my dear. I didn't save you just to kill you."

"I thank you, stranger," she said, "but keep your distance anyway."

Despite the warning, he took two steps toward her. Then she knew who he was. No one else in Sanctuary stank so of rancid butter.

"Smhee," she said, equally softly.

He chuckled. "I know you can't see my face. So, though it's against my religious convictions, I will have to take a bath and quit smearing my body and hair with butter. I am as silent as a shadow, but what good is that talent when anyone can smell me a block away?"

Keeping her eyes on him, she stopped and cleaned her dagger on the dead man's robe.

"Are you the one who's been following me?" she said. She straightened up.

He hissed with surprise, then said, "You saw me?"

"No. But I knew someone was dogging me."

"Ah! You have a sixth sense. Or a guilty conscience. Come! Let's get away before someone comes along."

"I'd like to know who these men are . . . were."

"They're Raggah," Smhee said. "There are two others fifty yards from here, lookouts, I suppose. They'll be coming soon to find out why these two haven't shown up with you."

That shocked her even more than the attack.

"You mean the purple mage wants *me*? Why?"

"I do not know. Perhaps he thinks as so many others do. That is, that Benna told you more than you have said he did. But come! Quickly!"

"Where?"

"To your place. We can talk there, can't we?"

They walked swiftly toward her building.

Smhee kept looking back, but the place where they had killed the two men was no longer visible. When they got to the door, however, she stopped.

"If I knock on the door for the keeper, the Raggah might hear it," she whispered. "But I have to get in. My daughter is very sick. She needs the medicine I got from Doctor Nadeesh."

"So that's why you were at his home," Smhee said. "Very well. You bang on the door. I'll be the rearguard."

He was suddenly gone, moving astonishingly swift and silently for such a fat man. But his aroma lingered.

She did as he suggested, and presently Shmurt came grumbling to the door and unbolted it. Just as she stepped in she smelled the butter more strongly, and Smhee was inside and pushing the door shut before the startled doorkeeper could protest.

"He's all right," Ma'sha said.

Old Shmurt peered with runny eyes at Smhee by the light of his oil lamp. Even with good vision, however, Shmurt couldn't see Smhee's face. It was covered with a green mask.

Shmurt looked disgusted.

"I know your husband isn't much," he croaked. "But taking up with this foreigner, this tub of rotten butter . . . *shewaw!*"

"It's not what you think," she said indignantly.

Smhee said, "I *must* take a bath. Everyone

knows me at once."

"Is Eevroen home?" Masha said.

Shmurt snorted and said, "At this early hour? No, you and your stinking lover will be safe."

"Dammit!" Masha said. "He's here on business!"

"Some business!"

"Mind your tongue, you old fart!" Masha said. "Or I'll cut it out!"

Shmurt slammed the door to his room behind him. He called, "Whore! Slut! Adulteress!"

Masha shrugged, lit her lamp, and went up the steps with Smhee close behind her. Wallu looked very surprised when the fat man came in with her daughter.

"Who is this?"

"Someone *can't* identify me?" Smhee said. "Does she have a dead nose?"

He removed his mask.

"She doesn't get out much," Masha said. She hurried to Kheem, who lay sleeping on her rag pile. Smhee took off his cloak, revealing thin arms and legs and a body like a ball of cheese. His shirt and vest, made of some velvety material speckled with glittering sequins, clung tightly to his trunk. A broad leather belt encircled his paunch, and attached to it were two scabbards containing knives, a third from which poked the end of a bamboo pipe, and a leather bag about the size of Masha's head. Over one shoulder and the side of his neck was coiled a thin rope.

"Tools of the trade," he said in answer to Masha's look.

Masha wondered what the trade was, but she didn't have time for him. She felt Kheem's forehead and pulse, then went to the water pitcher on the ledge in the corner.

After mixing the powder with the water as Nadeesh had instructed and pouring out some into a large spoon, she turned. Smhee was on his knees by the child and reaching into the bag on his belt.

"I have some talent for doctoring," he said as she came to his side. "Here. Put that quack's medicine away and use this."

He stood up and held out a small leather envelope. She just looked at him.

"Yes, I know you don't want to take a chance with a stranger. But please believe me. This green powder is a thousand times better than that placebo Nadeesh gave you. If it doesn't cure the child, I'll cut my throat. I promise you."

"Much good that'd do the baby," Wallu said.

"Is it a magical potion?" Masha said.

"No. Magic might relieve the symptoms, but the disease would still be there, and when the magic wore off, the sickness would return. Here. Take it! I don't want you two to say a word about it, ever, but I was once trained in the art of medicine. And where I come from, a doctor is twenty times superior to any you'll find in Sanctuary."

Masha studied his dark shiny face. He looked as if he might be about forty years old. The high broad forehead, the long straight nose, the well-shaped mouth would have made him handsome if his cheeks weren't so thick and his jowls so baggy. Despite his fatness, he looked intelligent; the black eyes below the thick bushy eyebrows were keen and lively.

"I can't afford to experiment with Kheem," she said.

He smiled, perhaps an acknowledgment that he detected the uncertainty in her voice.

"You can't afford not to," he said. "If you don't use this, your child will die. And the longer you hesitate, the closer she gets to death. Every second counts."

Masha took the envelope and returned to the water pitcher. She set the spoon down without spilling its contents and began working as Smhee called out to her his instructions. He stayed with Kheem, one hand on her forehead, the other on her chest. Kheem breathed rapidly and shallowly.

Wallu protested. Masha told her to shut up more harshly than she'd intended. Wallu bit her lip and glared at Smhee.

Kheem was propped up by Smhee, and Masha got her to swallow the greenish water. Ten minutes or so later, the fever began to go down. An hour later, according to the sandglass, she was given another spoonful. By dawn, she seemed to be rid of it, and she was sleeping peacefully.

Meantime, Masha and Smhee talked in low tones. Wallu had gone to bed, but not to sleep, shortly before sunrise. Eevroen had not appeared. Probably he was sleeping off his liquor in an empty crate on the wharf or in some doorway. Masha was glad. She had been prepared to break another basin over his head if he made a fuss and disturbed Kheem.

Though she had seen the fat little man a number of times, she did not know much about him. Nobody else did either. It was certain that he had first appeared in Sanctuary six weeks (sixty days) ago. A mercant ship of the Banmalts people had brought him, but this indicated little about his origin since the ship ported at many lands and islands.

Smhee had quickly taken a room on the second floor of a building, the first of which was occupied by the Khabeeber or "Diving Bird" Tavern. (The proprietor had jocularly named it thus because he claimed that his customers dived as deeply into alcohol for surcease as the *khabeeber* did into the ocean for fish.) He did no work nor was he known to thieve or mug. He seemed to have enough money for his purposes, whatever they were, but then he lived frugally. Because he smeared his body and hair with rancid butter, he was called "The Stinking Butterball" or "Old Rotten," though not to his face. He spent time in all the taverns and also was often seen in the farmers' market and the bazaar. As far as was known, he had shown no sexual interest in men or women or children. Or, as one wag put it, "not even in goats."

His religion was unknown though it was rumored that he kept an idol in a small wooden case in his room.

Now, sitting on the floor by Kheem, making the child drink water every half-hour, Masha questioned Smhee. And he in turn questioned her.

"You've been following me around," Masha said. "Why?"

"I've also investigated other women."

"You didn't say why."

"One answer at a time. I have something to do here, and I need a woman to help me. She has to be quick and strong and very brave and intelligent. And desperate."

He looked around the room as if anybody who lived in it had to be desperate indeed.

"I know your history," he said. "You came from a fairly well-to-do family, and as a child you lived in the Eastern quarter. You were not born and bred in the Maze, and you want to get out of it. You've worked hard, but you just are not going to succeed in your ambition. Not unless something unusual comes

your way and you have the courage to seize it,
no matter what the consequences might be."

"This has to do with Benna and the jewel,
doesn't it?" she said.

He studied her face by the flickering light of
the lamp.

"Yes."

He paused.

"And the purple mage."

Masha sucked in a deep breath. Her heart
thudded far more swiftly than her fatigue
could account for. A coldness spread from her
toes to the top of her head, a not unpleasant
coldness.

"I've watched in the shadows near your
building," he said. "Many a night. And two
nights ago I saw the Raggah steal into other
shadows and watch the same window. Fortunately, you did not go out during that time to
midwife. But tonight . . . ."

"Why would the Raggah be interested in
me?"

He smiled slowly.

"You're smart enough to guess why. The
mage thinks you know more than you let on
about the jewel. Or perhaps he thinks Benna
told you more than you've repeated."

He paused again, then said, "Did he?"

"Why should I tell you if he did?"

"You owe me for your life. If that isn't
enough to make you confide in me, consider
this. I have a plan whereby you can not only
be free of the Maze, you can be richer than

any merchant, perhaps richer than the governor himself. You will even be able to leave Sanctuary, to go to the capital city itself. Or anywhere in the world."

She thought, if Benna could do it, we can.

But then Benna had not gotten away.

She said, "Why do you need a woman? Why not another man?"

Smhee was silent for a long time. Evidently, he was wondering just how much he should tell her. Suddenly, he smiled, and something invisible, an unseen weight seemed to fall from him. Somehow, he even looked thinner.

"I've gone this far," he said. "So I must go all the way. No backing out now. The reason I must have a woman is that the mage's sorcery has a weakness. His magical defenses will be set up to repel men. He will not have prepared them against women. It would not occur to him that a woman would try to steal his treasure. Or . . . kill him."

"How do you know that?"

"I don't think it would be wise to tell you that now. You must take my word for it. I do know far more about the purple mage than anyone else in Sanctuary."

"You might, and that still wouldn't be much," she said.

"Let me put it another way. I do know much about him. More than enough to make me a great danger to him."

"Does he know much about you?"

Smhee smiled again. "He doesn't know I'm

here. If he did, I'd be dead by now."

They talked until dawn, and by then Masha was deeply committed. If she failed, then her fate would be horrible. And the lives of her daughters and her mother would become even worse. Far worse. But if she continued as she had, she would be dooming them anyway. She might die of a fever or be killed, and then they would have no supporter and defender.

Anyway, as Smhee pointed out, though he didn't need to, the mage was after her. Her only defense was a quick offense. She had no other choice except to wait like a dumb sheep and be slaughtered. Except that, in this situation, the sheep would be tortured before being killed.

Smhee knew what he was saying when he had said that she was desperate.

When the wolf's tail, the false dawn, came, she rose stiffly and went through to her room and looked out the window. Not surprisingly, the corpses of the Raggah were gone.

Shortly thereafter, Kheem awoke, bright-eyed, and asked for food. Masha covered her with kisses, and, weeping joyfully, prepared breakfast. Smhee left. He would be back before noon. But he gave her five *shaboozh* and some lesser coin. Masha wakened her mother, gave her the money, and told her that she would be gone for a few days. Wallu wanted to question her, but Masha told her sternly that she would be better off if she knew no more than she did now.

"If Eevroen wants to know where I am, tell him that I have been called to help deliver a rich farmer's baby. If he asks for the man's name, tell him it is Shkeedur sha-Mizl. He lives far out and only comes into town twice a year except on special business. It doesn't matter that it's a lie. By the time I get back— it'll be soon—we'll be leaving at once. Have everything we'll need for a long journey packed into that bag. Just clothes and eating utensils and the medicine. If Kheem has a relapse, give her Smhee's powders."

Wallu wailed then, and Masha had to quiet her down.

"Hide the money. No! Leave one *shaboozh* where Eevroen will find it when he looks for money. Conceal the rest where he can't find it. He'll take the *shaboozh* and go out to drink, and you won't be bothered with him or his questions."

When the flaming brass bowl of the noon sun had reached its apex, Smhee came. His eyes looked very red, but he didn't act fatigued. He carried a carpet bag from which he produced two dark cloaks, two robes, and the masks which the priests of Shalpa wore in public.

He said, "How did you get rid of your

mother and the children?"

"A neighbor is keeping the children until mother gets back from shopping," she said. "Eevroen still hasn't shown up."

"Nor will he for a long time," Smhee said. "I dropped a coin as I passed him staggering this way. He snatched it, of course, and ran off to a tavern.

"The *Swordfish* will be leaving port in three days. I've arranged for passage on her and also to be hidden aboard her if her departure is delayed. I've been very busy all morning."

"Including taking a bath," she said.

"You don't smell too good yourself," he said. "But you can bathe when we get to the river. Put these on."

She went into her room, removed her clothes, and donned the priest's garb. When she came out, Smhee was fully dressed. The bag attached to his belt bulged beneath his cloak.

"Give me your old clothes," he said. "We'll cache them outside the city, though I don't think we'll be needing them."

She did so, and he stuffed them into the belt-bag.

"Let's go," he said.

She didn't follow him to the door. He turned and said, "What's the matter? Your liver getting cold?"

"No," she said. "Only . . . mother's very short-sighted. I'm afraid she'll be cheated when she buys the food."

He laughed and said something in a foreign tongue.

"For the sake of Igil! When we return, we'll have enough to buy out the farmers' market a thousand times over!"

"If we get back . . . ." she murmured. She wanted to go to Looza's room and kiss the children goodbye. But that was not wise. Besides, she might lose her determination if she saw them now.

They walked out while old Shmurt stared. He was the weakest point in their alibi, but they hoped they wouldn't need any. At the moment, he was too dumbfounded at seeing them to say anything. And he would be afraid to go to the soldiers about this. He probably was thinking that two priests had magically entered the house, and it would be indiscreet to interfere in their business.

Thirty minutes later, they mounted the two horses which Smhee had arranged to be tied to a tree outside city limits.

"Weren't you afraid they'd be stolen?" she said.

"There are two stout fellows hidden in the grass near the river," he said. He waved toward it, and she saw two men come from it. They waved back and started to walk back to the city.

There was a rough road along the White Foal River, sometimes coming near the stream, sometimes bending far away. They rode over it for three hours, and then Smhee said, "There's an old adobe building a quarter-mile inland. We'll sleep there for a while. I don't know about you, but I'm weary."

She was glad to rest. After hobbling the horses near a stand of the tall brown desert grass, they lay down in the midst of the ruins. Smhee went to sleep at once. She worried about her family for a while, and suddenly she was being shaken by Smhee. Dawn was coming up.

They ate some dried meat and bread and fruit and then mounted again. After watering the horses and themselves at the river, they rode at a canter for three more hours. And then Smhee pulled up on the reins. He pointed at the trees a quarter-mile inland. Beyond, rearing high, were the towering cliffs on the other side of the river. The trees on this side, however, prevented them from seeing the White Foal.

"The boat's hidden in there," he said. "Unless someone's stolen it. That's not likely, though. Very few people have the courage to go near the Isle of Shugthee."

"What about the hunters who bring down the furs from the north?"

"They hug the eastern shore, and they only go by in daylight. Fast."

They crossed the rocky ground, passing some low-growing purplish bushes and some irontrees with grotesquely twisted branches. A rabbit with long ears dashed by them,

causing her horse to rear up. She controlled
it, though she had not been on a horse since
she was eleven. Smhee said that he was glad
that it hadn't been his beast. All he knew
about riding was the few lessons he'd taken
from a farmer after coming to Sanctuary.
He'd be happy if he never had to get on
another one.

The trees were perhaps fifteen or twenty
deep from the river's edge. They dismounted,
removed the saddles, and hobbled the beasts
again. Then they walked through the tall cane-
like plants, brushing away the flies and other
pestiferous insects, until they got to the
stream itself. Here grew stands of high reeds,
and on a hummock of spongy earth was
Smhee's boat. It was a dugout which could
hold only two.

"Stole it," Smhee said without offering any
details.

She looked through the reeds down the
river. About a quarter of a mile away, the
river broadened to become a lake about two
and a half miles across. In its center was the
Isle of Shugthee, a purplish mass of rock.
From this distance, she could not make out its
details.

Seeing it, she felt coldness ripple over her.

"I'd like to take a whole day and a night to
scout it," he said. "So you could become
familiar with it, too. But we don't have time.
However, I can tell you everything I know. I
wish I knew more."

She doffed her clothes and bathed in the river while Smhee unhobbled the horses and took them some distance up to let them drink. When she came back, she found him just returning with them.

"Before dusk comes, we'll have to move them down to a point opposite the isle," he said. "And we'll saddle them, too."

They left the horses to go to a big boulder outside the trees but distant from the road. At its base was a hollow large enough for them to lie down in. Here they slept, waking now and then to talk softly or to eat a bite or to go behind the rock and urinate. The insects weren't so numerous here as in the trees, but they were bad enough.

Not once, as far as they knew, did anyone pass on the road.

When they walked the horses down the road, Smhee said, "You've been very good about not asking questions, but I can see you're about to explode with curiosity. You have no idea who the purple mage really is. Not unless you know more than the other Sancturians."

"All I know," she said, "is that they say that the mage came here about ten years ago. He came with some hired servants, and many boxes, some small, some large. No one knew what his native land was, and he didn't stay long in town. One day he disappeared with the servants and the boxes. It was some time before people found out that he'd moved into

the caves of the Isle of Shugthee. Nobody had
ever gone there because it was said that it was
haunted by the ghosts of the Shugthee. They
were a little hairy people who inhabited this
land long before the first city of the ancients
was built here."

"How do you know he's a mage?" Smhee
said.

"I don't, but everybody says he is. Isn't he?"

"He is," Smhee said, looking grim.

"Anyway, he sent his servants in now and
then to buy cattle, goats, pigs, chickens,
horses, vegetables, and animal feed and fruit.
These were men and women from some
distant land. Not from his, though. And then
one day they ceased coming in. Instead, the
Raggah came. From that day on, no one has
seen the servants who came with the mage."

"He probably got rid of them," Smhee said.
"He may have found some reason to distrust
them. Or no reason at all."

"The fur trappers and hunters who've gone
by the isle say they've seen some strange
things. Hairy beast-faced dwarfs. Giant
spiders."

She shuddered.

"Benna died of spider bites," Smhee said.

The fat little man reached into his belt-bag
and brought out a metal jar. He said, "Before
we leave in the boat tonight we'll rub the
ointment in this on us. It will repel some of
the spiders but not, unfortunately, all."

"How do you know that?"

"I know."

They walked silently for a while. Then he sighed, and said, "We'll get bitten. That is certain. Only . . . all the spiders that will bite us—I hope so, anyway—won't be real spiders. They'll be products of the mage's magic. Apparitions. But apparitions that can kill you just as quickly or as slowly and usually as painfully as the real spiders."

He paused, then said, "Benna probably died from their bites."

Masha felt as if she were turning white under her dark skin. She put her hands on his arm.

"But . . . but . . . !"

"Yes, I know. If the spiders were not real, then why should they harm him? That is because he thought they were real. His mind did the rest to him."

She didn't like it that she couldn't keep her voice from shaking.

"How can you tell which is real and which magical?"

"In the daylight the unreal spiders look a little transparent. By that I mean that if they stand still, you can see dimly through them. But then they don't stand still much. And we'll be in the dark of night. So . . . .

"Look here, Masha. You have to be strong stuff to go there. You have to overcome your fear. A person who lets fear conquer him or her is going to die even if he knows that the spider is unreal. He'll make the sting of the

bite himself and the effects of the venom. And
he'll kill himself. I've seen it happen in my
native land."

"But you say that we might get bitten by a
real spider. How can I tell which is which in
the dark?"

"It's a problem."

He added after a few seconds, "The ointment should repulse most of the real spiders.
Maybe, if we're lucky. You see, we have an
advantage that Benna didn't have. I know
what faces us because I come from the mage's
land. His true name is Kemren, and he
brought with him the real spiders and some
other equally dangerous creatures. They
would have been in some of the boxes. I am
prepared for them, and so will you be. Benna
wasn't, and any of these Sanctuary thieves
will get the same fate."

Masha asked why Kemren had come here.
Smhee chewed on his lower lip for a while
before answering.

"You may as well know it all. Kemren was a
priest of the goddess Weda Krizhtawn of the
island of Sherranpip. That is far east and
south of here, though you may have heard of
it. We are a people of the water, of lakes,
rivers, and the sea. Weda Krizhtawn is the
chief goddess of water, and she has a mighty
temple with many treasures near the sea.

"Kemren was one of the higher priests, and
he served her well for years. In return, he was
admitted into the inner circle of mages and

taught both black and white magic. Though, actually, there is little difference between the two branches, the main distinction being whether the magician uses his powers for good or evil.

"And it isn't always easy to tell what is good and what is evil. If a mage makes a mistake, and his use turns out to be for evil, even if he sincerely thought it was for good, then there is a . . . backlash. And the mage's character becomes changed for the worse in proportion to the amount of magical energy used."

He stopped walking.

"We're opposite the isle now."

It wasn't visible from the road. The plain sloped upward from the road, becoming a high ridge near the river. The tall spreading blackish *hukharran* bush grew on top of it. They walked the horses up the ridge, where they hobbled them near a pool of rainwater. The beasts began cropping the long brownish grass that grew among the bushes.

The isle was in the center of the lake and seemed to be composed mostly of a purplish rock. It sloped gently from the shore until near the middle, where a series of peculiar formations formed a spine. The highest prominence was a monolith perforated near its top as if a tunnel had been carved through it.

"The camel's eye Benna spoke of," Smhee said. "Over there is the formation known as the ape's head, and at the other end is that which the natives call the dragon's tail."

On the edge of the isle grew some trees, and in the waters by it were the ubiquitous tall reeds.

There was no sight or sound of life on it. Even the birds seemed to shun it.

"But I floated down past it at night several times," he said, "and I could hear the lowing of some cattle and the braying of a donkey. Also, I heard a weird call, but I don't know if it was from a bird or an animal. And I heard a peculiar grunting sound, but it wasn't from pigs."

"That camel's eye looks like a good place for a sentry," she said. "I got the impression from Benna that that is where he entered the caves. It must've been a very dangerous climb, especially during the dark."

"Benna was a good man," Smhee said. "But he wasn't prepared enough. There are eyes watching now. Probably through holes in the rocks. From what I heard, the mage had his servants buy a number of excavating tools. He would have used them to enlarge the caves and to make tunnels to connect the caves."

She took a final look in the sunlight at the sinister purple mass and turned away.

Night had come. The winds had died down. The sky was cloudy, but the covering was thin. The full moon glowed through some of these, and now and then broke through. The nightbirds made crazy startling sounds. The mosquitoes hummed around them in dense masses, and if it hadn't been for Smhee's ointment would have driven them out of the trees within a few minutes. Frogs croaked in vast chorus; things plopped into the water.

They shoved the boat out to the edge of the reeds and climbed in. They wore their cloaks now but would take them off when they got to the isle. Masha's weapons were a dagger and a short thin sword used for thrusting only.

They paddled silently as possible, the current helping their rate of speed, and presently the isle loomed darkly to their right. They landed halfway down the eastern shore and dragged the dugout slowly to the nearest tree.

They put their cloaks in the boat, and Masha placed a coil of rope over her shoulder and neck.

The isle was quiet. Not a sound. Then came a strange grunting cry followed by a half-moaning, half-squalling sound. Her neck iced.

"Whatever that is," Smhee said, "it's no spider."

He chuckled as if he were making a joke.

They'd decided—what else could they do?—that the camel's eye would be too heavily guarded after Benna's entrance through it. But there had to be more accessible places to get in. These would be guarded, too, especially since they must have been made more security-conscious by the young thief.

"What I'd like to find is a secret exit," Smhee said. "Kemren must have one, perhaps more. He knows that there might come a time when he'll be sorely in need of it. He's a crafty bastard."

Before they'd taken the boat, Smhee had revealed that Kemren had fled Sherranpip with many of the temple's treasures. He had also taken along spider's eggs and some of the temple's animal guardians.

"If he was a high priest," Masha had said, "why would he do that? Didn't he have power and wealth enough?"

"You don't understand our religion," the fat thief had said. "The priests are surrounded by treasures that would pop your eyes out of their sockets if you saw them. But the priests themselves are bound by vows to extreme poverty, to chastity, to a harsh bare life. Their reward is the satisfaction of serving Weda Krizhtawn and her people. It wasn't enough for Kemren. He must have become evil while performing some magic that went wrong. He is the first priest ever to commit such a blasphemy.

"And I, a minor priest, was selected to track him down and to make him pay for his crime. I've been looking for him for thirteen years. During that time, to effect the vengeance of Weda Krizhtawn, I have had to break some of my own vows and to commit crimes which I must pay for when I return to my land."

"Won't she pardon you for these because

you have done them in her name?" Masha had said.

"No. She accepts no excuses. She will thánk me for completing my mission, but I must still pay. Look at me. When I left Sherranpip, I was as skinny as you. I led a very exemplary life. I ate little, I slept in the cold and rain, I begged for my food, I prayed much. But during the years of my crimes and the crimes of my years, I have eaten too well so that Kemren, hearing of the fat fellow, would not recognize me. I have been reeling drunk, I have gambled—a terrible sin—I have fought with fists and blade, I have taken human lives, I . . . ."

He looked as if he were going to weep.

Masha said, "But you didn't quit smearing yourself with butter?"

"I should have, I should have!" he cried. "But, apart from lying with women, that is the one thing I could not bring myself to do, though it was the first I should have done! And I'll pay for that when I get home, even though that is the hardest thing for a priest to do! Even Kemren, I have heard, though he no longer worships Weda Krizhtawn, still butters himself!

"And the only reason I quit doing that is that I'm sure that he's conditioned his real spiders, and his guardian animals, to attack anyone who's covered with butter. That way he can make sure or thinks he can make sure, that no hunter of him will ever be able to get close. That is why, though it almost killed me with shame and guilt, I bathed this morning!"

Masha would have laughed if she hadn't felt so sorry for him. That was why his eyes had looked so red when he'd shown up at her apartment after bathing. It hadn't been fatigue but tears that had done it.

They drew their weapons, Masha a short sword and Smhee a long dagger. They set out for the base of the ridge of formations that ran down the center of the isle like serrations on a dragon's back. Before they'd gone far, Smhee put a restraining hand on her arm.

"There's a spider's web just ahead. Between those two bushes. Be careful of it. But look out for other dangers, since one will be obvious enough to distract your attention from others. And don't forget that the thorns of these bushes are probably poisonous."

In the dim moonlight she saw the web. It was huge, as wide as the stretch of her arms. She thought, if it's so big, what about its spinner?

It seemed empty, though. She turned to her left and walked slowly, her head turned to watch it.

Then something big scuttled out from under the bush at her. She stifled her scream and leaped toward the thing instead of following her desire to run away from it. Her sword leaped out as the thing sprang, and it spitted itself. Something soft touched the back of her hand. The end of a waving leg.

Smhee came up behind it as she stood there holding the sword out as far as she could to keep the arachnid away. Her arm got heavy with its weight, and slowly the blade sank toward the ground. The fat man slashed the thing's back open with his dagger. A foul odor vented from it. He brought his foot down on a leg and whispered, "Pull your sword out! I'll keep it pinned!"

She did so and then backed away. She was breathing very hard.

He jumped up and came down with both feet on the creature. Its legs waved for a while longer, but it was dying if not already dead.

"That was a real spider," he said, "although I suppose you know that. I suspect that the false spiders will be much smaller.

"Why?" she said. She wished her heart would quit trying to leap up through her throat.

"Because making them requires energy, and it's more effective to make a lot of little spiders and costs less energy than to make a few big ones. There are other reasons which I won't explain just now."

"Look out!" she cried, far louder than she should have. But it had been so sudden and had taken her off guard.

Smhee whirled and slashed out, though he hadn't seen the thing. It bounded over the web, its limbs spread out against the dimness, its great round ears profiled. It came down growling, and it fell upon Smhee's blade. This

was no man's-headsized spider but a thing as
big as a large dog and furry and stinking of
something—monkey?—and much more vital
than the arachnid. It bore Smhee backward
with his weight; he fell on the earth.

Snarling, it tried to bury its fangs in
Smhee's throat. Masha broke from her par-
alysis and thrust with a fury and strength
that only fear could provide. The blade went
through its body. She leaped back, drawing it
out, and then lunged again. This time the
point entered its neck.

Smhee, gasping, rolled it off him and stood
up. He said, "By Wishvu's whiskers! I've got
blood all over me. A fine mess! Now the
others will smell me!"

"What is it?" Masha said shakily.

"A temple guardian ape. Actually, it's not an
ape but a very large tailless monkey. Kemren
must have brought some cubs with him."

Masha got close to the dead beast, which
was lying on its back. The open mouth showed
teeth like a leopard's.

"They eat meat," he said. "Unlike other
monkeys, however, they're not gregarious.
Our word for them, translated, would be the
solitary ape."

Masha wondered if one of Smhee's duties
had been teaching. Even under these circumstances, he had to be pedantic.

He looked around. "Solitary or not, there
are probably a number on this isle."

After dragging the two carcasses into the

river, they proceeded cautiously. Smhee looked mostly ahead; Masha, behind. Both looked to both sides of them. They came to the base of the ridges of rock. Smhee said, "The animal pens are north. That's where I heard them as I went by in the boat. I think we should stay away from them. If they scent us and start an uproar, we'll have the Raggah out and on our asses very quickly."

Smhee stopped suddenly, and said, "Hold it!"

Masha looked around quickly. What had he seen or heard?

The fat man got down on his knees and pushed against the earth just in front of him.

He rose and said, "There's a pit under that firm-looking earth. I felt it give way as I put my foot on it. That's why it pays not to walk swiftly here."

They circled it, Smhee testing each step before taking another. Masha thought that if they had to go this slowly, they would take all night before they got to the ridge. But then he led her to a rocky place, and she breathed easier. However, he said, "They could carve a pit in the stone and put a pivoting lid over it."

She said, "Why are we going this way? You said the entrances are on the north end."

"I said that I only observed people entering on the north end. But I also observed something very interesting near here. I want to check it out. It may be nothing for us, but again . . . ."

Still moving slowly but faster than on the earth, they came to a little pool. It was about ten feet in diameter, a dark sheet of water on which bubbles appeared and popped. Smhee crouched down and stared at its sinister-looking surface.

She started to whisper a question, but he said, "Shh!"

Presently, something scuttled with a clatter across the solid rock from the shore. She jumped but uttered no exclamation. The thing looked like a spider in the dark, an enormous one, larger than the one they'd killed. It paid no attention to them or perhaps it wasn't at all aware of them. It leaped into the pool and disappeared. Smhee said, "Let's get behind that boulder."

When they were in back of it, she said, "What's going on?"

"When I was spying, I saw some things going into and coming out of this hole. It was too far away to see what they were, though I suspected they were giant spiders or perhaps crabs."

"So?"

His hand gripped her wrist.

"Wait!"

The minutes oozed by like snails. Mosquitoes hummed around them, birds across the river called, and once she heard, or thought she heard, that peculiar half-grunt, half-squall. And once she started when something splashed in the river. A fish. She hoped that was all it was.

Smhee said softly, "Ah!"

He pointed at the pool. She strained her eyes and then saw what looked like a swelling of the water in its center. The mound moved toward the edge of the pool, and then it left the water. It clacked as it shot toward the river. Soon another thing came and then another, and all of a sudden at least twenty popped up and clattered across the rocks.

Smhee finally relieved her bursting question.

"They look like the *bengil* crab of Sherran-pip. They live in that hole but they must catch fish in the river."

"What is that to us?"

"I think the pool must be an entrance to a cave. Or caves. The crabs are not water-breathers."

"Are they dangerous?"

"Only when in water. On land they'll either run or, if cornered, try to defend themselves. They aren't poisonous, but their claws are very powerful."

He was silent for a moment, then said, "The mage is using them to defend the entrance to a cave, I'm sure. An entrance which is also an exit. For him as well as for the crabs. That pool has to be one of his secret escape routes."

Masha thought, "Oh, no!" and she rolled her eyes. Was this fat fool really thinking about trying to get inside through the pool?

"How could the mage get out this way if the crabs would attack him?"

"He would throw poisoned meat to them. He could do any number of things. What matters just now is that he wouldn't have bothered to bring their eggs along from Sherranpip unless he had a use for them. Nor would he have planted them here unless he needed them to guard this pool. Their flesh is poisonous to all living things except the *ghoondah* fish."

He chuckled. "But the mage has outsmarted himself. If I hadn't noticed the *bengil*, I would never have considered that pool as an entrance."

While he had been whispering, another group had emerged and run for the river. He counted them, thirty in all.

"Now is the time to go in," he said. "They'll all be feeding. That crab you first saw was their scout. It found a good place for catching fish, determined that there wasn't any enemy around, and returned with the good news. In some ways, they're more ant than crab. Fortunately, their nests aren't as heavily populated as an anthole."

He said, however, that they should wait a few minutes to make sure that all had left. "By all, I mean all but a few. There are always a few who stay behind to guard the eggs."

"Smhee, we'll drown!"

"If other people can get out through the pool, then we can get in."

"You don't know for sure that the pool is an escape route! What if the mage put the crabs there for some other reason?"

"What if? What if? I told you this would be very dangerous. But the rewards are worth the risk."

She stiffened. That strange cry had come again. And it was definitely nearer.

"It may be hunting us," Smhee said. "It could have smelled the blood of the ape."

"What is it?" she said, trying to keep her teeth from chattering.

"I don't know. We're downwind from it, but it sounds as if it'll soon be here. Good! That will put some stiffening in our backbone, heat our livers. Let's go now!"

So, he was scared, too. Somehow, that made her feel a little better.

They stuck their legs down into the chilly water. They found no bottom. Then Smhee ran around to the inland side and bent down. He probed with his hand around the edge.

"The rock goes about a foot down, then curves inward," he said. "I'll wager that this was once a pothole of some sort. When Kemren came here, he carved out tunnels to the cave it led to and then somehow filled it with river water."

He stood up. The low strange cry was definitely closer now. She thought she saw something huge in the darkness to the north, but it could be her imagination.

"Oh, Igil!" she said. "I have to urinate!"

"Do it in the water. If it smells your urine
on the land, it'll know a human's been here.
And it might call others of its kind. Or make
such an uproar the Raggah will come."

He let himself down into the water and
clung to the stony edge.

"Get in! It's cold but not as cold as death!"

She let herself down to his side. She had to
bite her lip to keep from gasping with shock.

He gave her a few hurried instructions and
said, "May Weda Krizhtawn smile upon us!"

And he was gone.

She took a deep breath while she was considering getting out of the pool and running
like a lizard chased by a fox to the river and
swimming across it. But instead she dived,
and as Smhee had told her to do, swam close
to the ceiling of rock. She was blind here even
with her eyes open, and, though she thought
mostly about drowning, she had room to
think about the crabs.

Presently, when her lungs were about to
burst and her head rang and the violent urge
to get air was about to make her breathe, her
flailing hand was grasped by something. The
next instant, she was pulled into air.

There was darkness all about. Her gaspings
mingled with Smhee's.

He said, between the wheezings, "There's plenty of airspace between the water and the ceiling. I dived down and came up as fast as I could out of the water, and I couldn't touch the rock above."

After they'd recovered their wind, he said, "You tread water while I go back. I want to see how far back this space goes."

She didn't have to wait long. She heard his swimming—she hoped it was his and not something else—and she called out softly when he was near. He stopped and said, "There's plenty of air until just before the tunnel or cave reaches the pool. Then you have to dive under a downthrust ledge of rock. I didn't go back out, of course, not with that creature out there. But I'm sure my esti-mate of distance is right."

She followed him in the darkness until he said, "Here's another downthrust."

She felt where he indicated. The stone did not go more than six inches before ceasing.

"Does the rope or your boots bother you any?" he said. "If they're too heavy, get rid of them."

"I'm all right."

"Good. I'll be back soon—if things are as I think they are."

She started to call to him to wait for her, but it was too late. She clung to the rough stone with her fingertips, moving her legs now and then. The silence was oppressive; it rang in her ears. And once she gasped when something touched her thigh.

The rope and boots did drag her down, and she was thinking of at least getting rid of the rope when something struck her belly. She grabbed it with one hand to keep it from biting her and with the other reached for her dagger. She went under water of course, and then she realized that she wasn't being attacked. Smhee, diving back, had run into her.

Their heads cleared the surface. Smhee laughed.

"Were you as frightened as I? I thought sure a *bengil* had me!"

Gasping, she said, "Never mind. What's over there?"

"More of the same. Another airspace for perhaps a hundred feet. Then another down-cropping."

He clung to the stone for a moment. Then he said, "Have you noticed how fresh the air is? There's a very slight movement of it, too."

She had noticed but hadn't thought about it. Her experiences with watery caves was nil until now.

"I'm sure that each of these caves is connected to a hole which brings in fresh air from above," he said. "Would the mage have gone to all this trouble unless he meant to use this for escape?"

He did something. She heard him breathing heavily, and then there was a splash.

"I pulled myself up the rock and felt

around," he said. "There is a hole up there to let air from the next cave into this one. And I'll wager that there is a hole in the ceiling. But it must curve so that light doesn't come in. Or maybe it doesn't curve. If it were day above, we might see the hole."

He dived; Masha followed him. They swam ahead then, putting their right hands out from side to side to feel the wall. When they came to the next downcropping, they went through beneath it at once.

At the end of this cave they felt a rock ledge that sloped gently upward. They crawled out onto it. She heard him fumbling around and then he said, "Don't cry out. I'm lighting a torch."

The light nevertheless startled her. It came from the tip of a slender stick of wood in his hand. By its illumination she saw him apply it to the end of a small pine torch. This caught fire, giving them more area of vision. The fire on the stick went out. He put the stick back into the opened belt-bag.

"We don't want to leave any evidence we've been here," he said softly. "I didn't mention that this bag contains many things, including another waterproof bag. But we must hurry. The torch won't last long, and I've got just one more."

They stood up and moved ahead. A few feet beyond the original area first illuminated by the torch were some dark bulks. Boats. Twelve of them, with light wood frameworks and skin-coverings. Each could hold three people. By them were paddles.

Smhee took out a dagger and began ripping the skins. Masha helped him until only one boat was left undamaged.

He said, "There must be entrances cut into the stone sections dividing the caves we just came through. I'll wager they're on the left-hand side as you come in. Anyone swimming in would naturally keep to the right wall and so wouldn't see the archways. The ledges where the crabs nest must also be on the left. Remember that when we come back. But I'd better find out for sure. We want to know exactly how to get out when the time comes."

He set his torch in a socket in the front of the boat, and pushed the boat down the slope and into the water. While Masha held the narrow craft steady, he got into it. She stood on the shore, feeling lonely with all that darkness behind her while she watched him by the light of the brand. Within a few minutes he came back, grinning.

"I was right! There's an opening cut into the stone division. It's just high enough for a boat to pass through if you duck down."

They dragged the boat back up onto the ledge. The cave ended about a hundred feet from the water. To the right was a U-shaped entrance. By its side were piles of torches and flint and steel and punk boxes. Smhee lit two, gave one to Masha, and then returned to the edge of the ledge to extinguish his little one.

"I think the mage has put all his magic spiders inside the caves," he said. "They'd require too much energy to maintain on the outside. The further away they are from him, the more energy he has to use to maintain them. The energy required increases according to the square of the distance."

Masha didn't ask him what he meant by "square."

"Stick close to me. Not just for your sake. For mine also. As I said, the mage will not have considered women trying to get into his place, so his powers are directed against men only. At least, I hope they are. That way he doesn't have to use as much energy on his magic."

"Do you want me to lead?" she said, hoping he wouldn't say yes.

"If you had as much experience as I, I wouldn't hesitate a moment. But you're still an apprentice. If we get out of here alive, you will be on your way to being a master."

They went up the steps cut out of the stone. At the top was another archway. Smhee stopped before it and held his torch high to look within it. But he kept his head outside it.

"Ha!"

He motioned her to come to his side. She saw that the interior of the deep doorway was grooved. Above the grooves was the bottom of a slab of stone.

"If the mechanism is triggered, that slab will crash down and block off anyone chasing the mage," he said. "And it'd crush anyone in the portal. Maybe . . . ."

He looked at the wall surrounding the archway but could find nothing.

"The release mechanism must be in the other room. A time-delay device."

He got as near to the entrance as he could without going into it, and he stuck his torch through the opening.

"I can't see it. It must be just around the corner. But I do see what looks like webs."

Masha breathed deeply.

"If they're real spiders, they'll be intimidated by the torches," he said. "Unless the mage has conditioned them not to be or uses magic to overcome their natural fear. The magic spiders won't pay any attention to the flame."

She thought that it was all very uncertain, but she did not comment.

He bent down and peered at the stone floor just beyond the doorway. He turned. "Here. Your young eyes are better than my old ones. Can you see a thread or anything like it raised above the floor just beyond the door?"

She said, "No, I can't."

"Nevertheless."

He threw his torch through the doorway. At his order, she got down with her cheek against the stone and looked against the flame.

She rose, saying, "I can see a very thin line about an inch above the floor. It could be a cord."

"Just as I thought. An old Sherranpip trick."

He stepped back after asking her to get out of the way. And he leaped through the doorway and came down past the cord. She followed. As they picked up their torches, he said pointing, "There are the mechanisms. One is the time-delay. The other releases the door so it'll fall behind the first who enters and trap him. Anyone following will be crushed by the slab."

After telling her to keep an eye on the rest of the room, he examined the array of wheels, gears, and counterweights and the rope that ran from one device through a hole in the ceiling.

"The rope is probably attached to an alarm system above," he said. "Very well. I know how to actuate both of these. If you should by any foul chance come back alone, all you have to do is to jump through and then throw a torch or something on that cord. The door will come down and block off your pursuers. But get outside as fast as you can because . . . ."

Masha said, "I know why."

"Good woman. Now, the spiders."

The things came before the webs were clearly visible in the light. She had expected to see the light reflected redly in their eyes, but they weren't. Their many eyes were huge and purplish and cold. They scuttled forward, waving the foremost pair of legs, then backed away as Smhee waved his torch at them. Masha walked half-turned away from him so that she could use the brand to scare away any attack from the rear or side.

Suddenly, something leaped from the edge of the darkness and soared toward her. She thrust the brand at it. But the creature seemed to go through the torch.

It landed on her arm and seized the hand that held the torch. She had clenched her teeth to keep from screaming if something like this happened. But she didn't even think of voicing her terror and disgust. She closed her hand on the body of the thing to crush it, and the fingers felt nothing.

The next moment, the spider disappeared.

She told Smhee what had happened.

"Thanks be to Klooshna!" he said. "You are invulnerable to them. If you weren't, you'd be swelling up now!"

"But what if it'd been a real spider?" she said as she kept waving her torch at the monsters that circled them. "I didn't know until my hand closed on it that it was not real."

"Then you'd be dying. But the fact that it ignored the brand showed you what it really was. You realized that even if you didn't think consciously about it."

They came to another archway. While she threw her torch through it and got down to look for another thread, Smhee held off the spiders.

"There doesn't seem to be any," she said.

"*Seem* isn't good enough," he said. "Hah, back, you creatures of evil! Look closely! Can you see any thin lines in the floor itself? Minute cracks?"

After a few seconds, she said, "Yes. They form a square."

"A trapdoor to drop us into a pit," he said. "You jump past it. And let's hope there isn't another trap just beyond it."

She said that she'd need a little run to clear the line. He charged the spiders, waving his torch furiously, and they backed away. When she called to him that she was safe, he turned and ran and leaped. A hairy, many-legged thing dashed through the entrance after him. Masha stepped up to the line and thrust her brand at it. It stopped. Behind it were masses that moved, shadows of solidity.

Smhee leaped toward the foremost one and jammed the burning red of his brand into the head. The stink of charred flesh assailed their nostrils. It ran backward but was stopped by those behind it. Then they retreated, and the thing, its eyes burned out, began running around and around, finally disappearing into the darkness. The others were now just beyond the doorway in the other cave. Smhee threw his torch into it.

"That'll keep them from coming through!" he said, panting. "I should have brought some extra torches, but even the greatest mind sometimes slips. Notice how the weight of those spiders didn't make the trapdoor drop? It must have a minimum limit. You only weigh eighty-five pounds. Maybe . . . ?"

"Forget it," she said.

"Right you are," he said, grinning. "But Masha, if you are to be a master thief, you must think of everything."

She thought of reminding him about the extra torches he'd forgotten but decided not to. They went on ahead through an enormous cavern and came to a tunnel. From its dark mouth streamed a stink like a newly opened tomb. And they heard the cry that was half-grunt, half-squall.

Smhee halted. "I hate to go into that tunnel. But we must. You look upward for holes in the ceiling, and I'll look everywhere else."

The stone, however, looked solid. When they were halfway down the bore, they were blasted with a tremendous growling and roaring.

"Lions?" Masha said.

"No. Bears."

At the opposite end were two gigantic animals, their eyes gleaming redly in the light, their fangs a dull white.

The two intruders advanced after waiting for the bears to charge. But these stayed by the doorway, though they did not cease their thunderous roaring nor their slashes at the air with their paws.

"The bears were making the strange cry," she said. "I've seen dancing bears in the bazaars, but I never heard them make a noise like that. Nor were they near as large."

He said, "They've got chains around their necks. Come on."

When they were within a few feet of the beasts, they stopped. The stench was almost overpowering now, and they were deafened by the uproar in the narrowness of the tunnel.

Smhee told her to hold her torch steady. He opened his belt-bag and pulled out two lengths of bamboo pipe and joined them. Then, from a small wooden case, he cautiously extracted a feathered dart. He inserted it in one and raised the blowpipe almost to his lips.

"There's enough poison on the tip of the dart to kill a dozen men," he said. "However, I doubt that it would do much harm, if any, if the dart sticks in their thick fat. So . . . ."

He waited a long time, the pipe now at his lips. Then, his cheeks swelled, and the dart shot out. The bear to the right, roaring even louder, grabbed at the missile stuck in its left eye. Smhee fitted another dart into the pipe and took a step closer. The monster on the left lunged against the restraining collar and chain. Smhee shot the second dart into its tongue.

The first beast struck fell to one side, its paws waving, and its roars subsided. The other took longer to become quiet, but presently both were snoring away.

"Let's hope they die," Smhee said. "I doubt we'll have time to shoot them again when we come back."

Masha thought that a more immediate concern was that the roaring might have alarmed the mage's servants.

They went through a large cavern, the floor of which was littered with human, cattle, and goat skeletons and bear dung. They breathed through their mouths until they got to an exit. This was a doorway which led to a flight of steps. At the top of the steps was another entrance with a closed massive wooden door. Affixed to one side was a great wooden bar.

"Another hindrance to pursuers," Smhee said. "Which will, in our case, be the Raggah."

After a careful inspection of the door, he gripped its handle and slowly opened it. Freshly oiled, it swung noiselessly. They went out into a very large room illuminated by six great torches at one end. Here streams of water ran out from holes in the ceiling and down wooden troughs and onto many wooden wheels set between metal uprights.

Against the right-hand side of the far wall was another closed door as massive as the first. It, too, could be barred shut.

Unlike the bare walls of the other caves, these were painted with many strange symbols.

"There's magic here," Smhee said. "I smell it."

He strode to the pool in which were set the wheels. The wheels went around and around impelled by the downpouring water. Masha counted aloud. Twelve.

"A magical number," Smhee said.

They were set in rows of threes. At one end of the axle of each were attached some gears which in turn were fixed to a shaft that ran into a box under the wheel. Smhee reached out to the nearest wheel from the pool edge and stopped it. Then he released it and opened the lid of the box beneath the wheel. Masha looked past him into the interior of the box. She saw a bewildering array of tiny gears and shafts. The shafts were connected to more gears at the axle end of tiny wheels on uprights.

Smhee stopped the wheel again and spun it against the force of the waterfall. The mechanism inside started working backward.

Smhee smiled. He closed the box and went to the door and barred it. He walked swiftly to the other side of the pool. There was a large box on the floor by it. He opened it and removed some metal pliers and wrenches.

"Help me get those wheels off their stands," he said.

"Why?"

"I'll explain while we work." He looked around. "Kemren would have done better to have set human guards here. But I suppose he thought that no one would ever get this far. Or, if they did, they'd not have the slightest idea what the wheels are for."

He told her what she was to do with the wheels, and they waded into the pool. The water only came to their ankles; a wide drain in the center ensured against overflow.

Masha didn't like being drenched, but she was sure that it would be worthwhile.

"These boxes contain devices which convert the mechanical power of the water-driven wheels to magical power," he said. "There are said to be some in the temple of Weda Krizhtawn, but I was too lowly to be allowed near them. However, I heard the high priests talking about them. They sometimes got careless in the presence of us lowly ones. Anyway, we were bound by vows to keep silent.

"I don't know exactly what these particular wheels are for. But they must be providing energy for whatever magic he's using. Part of the energy, anyway."

She didn't really understand what he was talking about, though she had an inkling. She worked steadily, ignoring the wetting, and removed a wheel. Then she turned it around and reattached it.

The wheel bore symbols on each of the paddles set along its rims. There were also symbols painted on its side.

Each wheel seemed to have the same symbols but in a different sequence.

When their work was done, Smhee said, "I don't know what their reversal will do. But I'll wager that it won't be for Kemren's good. We must hurry now. If he's sensitive to the inflow-outflow of his magic, he'll know something's wrong."

She thought that it would be better not to have aroused the mage. However, Smhee was the master; she, the apprentice.

Smhee started to turn away from the wheels but stopped.

"Look!"

His finger pointed at the wheels.

"Well?"

"Don't you see something strange?"

It was a moment before she saw what had made her uneasy without realizing why. No water was spilling from the paddles down to the pool. The water just seemed to disappear after striking them.

She looked wonderingly from them to him. "I see what you mean."

He spread out his hands. "I don't know what's happening. I'm not a mage or a sorcerer. But . . . that water has to be going someplace."

They put their boots back on, and he unshot

the bar of the door. It led to another flight of
steps, ending in another door. They went
down a corridor the walls of which were bare
stone. But there were also lit torches set in
brackets on them.

At the end of the corridor they came to a
round room. Light came down from torches;
the room was actually a tall shaft. Looking up
from the bottom, they could see a black
square outlined narrowly by bright light at its
top.

Voices came from above.

"It has to be a lift," Smhee whispered. He
said something in his native tongue that
sounded like a curse.

"We're stuck here until the lift comes
down."

He'd no sooner spoken than they heard a
squeal as of metal, and the square began
descending slowly.

"We're in luck!" Smhee said. "Unless
they're sending down men to see what's
happened to the wheels."

They retreated through the door at the
other end. Here they waited with their blades
ready. Smhee kept the door open a crack.

"There are only two. Both are carrying bags
and one has a haunch of meat. They're going

to feed the bears and the spiders!"

Masha wondered how the men intended to get past the bears to the arachnids. But maybe the bears attacked only strangers.

"One man has a torch," he said.

The door swung open, and a Raggah wearing a red-and-black striped robe stepped through. Smhee drove his dagger into the man's throat. Masha came out from behind the door and thrust her sword through the other man's neck.

After dragging the bodies into the room, they took off the robes and put them on.

"It's too big for me," she said. "I look ridiculous."

"Cut off the bottom," he said, but she had already started doing that.

"What about the blood on the robes?"

"We could wash it out, but then we'd look strange with dripping robes. We'll just have to take a chance."

They left the bodies lying on the floor and went back to the lift. This was an open-sided cage built of light (and expensive) imported bamboo. The top was closed, but it had a trap door. A rope descended through it.

They looked up but could see no one looking down.

Smhee pulled on the rope, and a bell clanged. No one was summoned by it, though.

"Whoever pulls this up is gone. No doubt he, or they, are not expecting the two to return so early. Well, we must climb up the pull-ropes. I hope you're up to it."

"Better than you, fat one," Masha said.

He smiled. "We'll see."

Masha, however, pulled herself up faster than he. She had to climb up onto the beam to which the wheel was attached and then crawl along it and swing herself down into the entrance. Smhee caught her as she landed on the edge, though she didn't need his help.

They were in a hallway the walls of which were hung with costly rugs and along which was expensive furniture. Oil lamps gave an adequate illumination.

"Now comes the hard part," he said between deep breaths. "There is a staircase at each end of this hall. Which leads to the mage?"

"I'd take that one," she said, pointing.

"Why?"

"I don't exactly know why. I just feel that it's the right one."

He smiled, saying, "That's as good a reason as any for me. Let's go."

Their hands against each other inside their voluminous sleeves, but holding daggers, the hoods pulled out to shadow their faces, they walked up the stairs. These curved to end in another hall, even more luxuriously furnished. There were closed doors along it, but Smhee wouldn't open them.

"You can wager that the mage will have a guard or guards outside his apartment."

They went up another flight of steps in time

to see the back of a Raggah going down the hall. At the corner, Masha looked around it. No one in sight. She stepped out, and just then a Raggah came around the corner at the right-hand end of the hall. She slowed, impercep-tibly, she hoped, then resumed her stride. She heard Smhee behind her saying, "When you get close, within ten feet of her, move quickly to one side."

She did so just as the Raggah, a woman, noticed the blood on the front of her robe. The woman opened her mouth, and Smhee's thrown knife plunged into her belly. She fell forward with a thump. The fat man withdrew his knife, wiped it on the robe, and they dragged her through a doorway. The room was unlit. They dropped her near the door and went out, closing it behind them.

They went down to the end of the hall from which the woman had come and looked around the corner. There was a very wide and high-ceilinged corridor there, and from a great doorway halfway down it came much light, many voices, and the odor of cooking. Masha hadn't realized until then how hungry she was; saliva ran in her mouth.

"The other way," Smhee said, and he trotted toward the staircase. At its top, Masha looked around the corner. Halfway down the length of this hall a man holding a spear stood before a door. By his side crouched a huge black wolfish dog on a leash.

She told Smhee what she'd seen.

As excited as she'd ever seen him, he said, "He must be guarding the mage's rooms!"

Then, in a calmer tone, "He isn't aware of what we've done. He must be with a woman or a man. Sexual intercourse, you know, drains more out of a person than just physical energy. Kemren won't be sensitive to the wheels just now."

Masha didn't see any reason to comment on that. She said, "The dog didn't notice me, but we can't get close before he alerts the guard."

Masha looked behind her. The hall was still empty. But what if the mage had ordered a meal to be delivered soon?

She told Smhee what she'd just thought. After a brief consultation, they went back down the stairs to the hall. There they got an exquisitely silver-chased tray and put some small painted dishes and gold pitchers on it. These they covered with a golden cloth, the worth of which was a thousand times more than Masha could make if she worked as dentist and midwife until she was a hundred years old.

With this assemblage, which they hoped would look like a late supper tray, they went to the hall. Masha had said that if the mage was with a sexual partner, it would look more authentic if they carried two trays. But even before Smhee voiced his objections, she had thought that he had to have his hands free. Besides, one tray clattering on the floor was bad enough, though its impact would be softened by the thick rug.

The guard seemed half-asleep, but the dog, rising to its feet and growling, fully awakened him. He turned toward them, though not without a glance at the other end of the hall first. Masha, in front of Smhee, walked as if she had a right to be there. The guard held the spear pointing at them in one hand and said something in his harsh back-of-the-throat speech.

Smhee uttered a string of nonsense syllables in a low but equally harsh voice. The guard said something. And then Masha stepped to one side, dropping the tray. She bent over, muttering something guttural, as if she were apologizing for her clumsiness.

She couldn't see Smhee, but she knew that he was snatching the blowpipe from his sleeve and applying it to his lips. She came up from her bent position, her sword leaping out of her scabbard, and she ran toward the dog. It bounded toward her, the guard having released the leash. She got the blade out from the leather just in time and rammed it into the dog's open mouth as it sprang soundlessly toward her throat. The blade drove deep into its throat, but she went backward from its weight and fell onto the floor.

The sword had been torn from her grip, but the dog was heavy and unmoving on her chest. She pushed him off though he must have weighed as much as she. She rolled over and got quickly, but trembling, to her feet. The guard was sitting down, his back against the wall. One hand clutched the dart stuck in his cheek. His eyes were open but glazing. In a few seconds the hand fell away. He slumped to one side, and his bowels moved noisily.

The dog lay with the upper length of the sword sticking from its mouth. His tongue extended from the jaws, bloody, seeming almost an independent entity, a stricken worm.

Smhee grabbed the bronze handle of the door.

"Pray for us, Masha! If he's barred the door on the inside . . . !"

The door swung open.

Smhee bounded in, the dead man's spear in his hands. Masha, following, saw a large room the air of which was green and reeking of incense. The walls were covered with tapestries, and the heavy dark furniture was ornately carved with demons' heads. They paused to listen and heard nothing except a faint burbling noise.

"Get the bodies in quickly!" Smhee said, and they dragged the corpses inside. They expected the dreaded mage to walk in at any time, but he still had not appeared when they shut the door.

Smhee whispered, "Anyone coming by will notice that there is no guard."

They entered the next room cautiously. This was even larger and was obviously the bedroom. The bed was huge and round and on a platform with three steps. It was covered with a rich scarlet material brocaded in gold.

"He must be working in his laboratory," Smhee whispered.

They slowly opened the door to the next room.

The burbling became louder then. Masha saw that it proceeded from a great glass vessel shaped like an upside-down cone. A black-green liquid simmered in it, and large bubbles rose from it and passed out the open end. Beneath it was a brazier filled with glowing coals. From the ceiling above a metal vent admitted the fumes.

The floor was mosaic marble in which were set pentagrams and nonagrams. From the center of one rose a wisp of evil-smelling smoke. A few seconds later, the smoke ceased.

There were many tables holding other mysterious equipment and racks holding long thick rolls of parchment and papyrus. In the middle of the room was a very large desk of some shiny reddish wood. Before it was a chair of the same wood, its arms and back carved with human-headed dragons.

The mage, clad in a purple silk robe which was embroidered with golden centaurs and gryphons, was in the chair. His face was on the desk, and his arms were spread out on it. He stank of rancid butter.

Smhee approached him slowly, then grabbed the thin curly hair of the mage's topknot and raised the head.

There was water on the desk, and water ran

from the dead man's nose and mouth.

"What happened to him?" she whispered.

Smhee did not reply at once. He lifted the body from the chair and placed it on the floor. Then he knelt and thumped the mage's chest. The fat man rose smiling.

"What happened is that the reversal of the wheels' motion caused the water which should have fallen off the paddles to go instead to the mage. The conversion of physical energy to magical energy was reversed."

He paused.

"The water went into the mage's body. He *drowned!*"

He raised his eyes and said, "Blessed is Weda Krizhtawn, the goddess of water! She has her revenge through her faithful servant, Rhandhee Ghee!"

He looked at Masha. "That is my true name, Rhandhee Ghee. And I have revenged the goddess and her worshippers. The defiler and thief is dead, and I can go home now. Perhaps she will forgive some of my sins because I have fulfilled her intent. I won't go to hell, surely. I will suffer in a purgatory for a while and then, cleansed with pain, will go to the lowest heaven. And then, perhaps . . . ."

"You forget that I am to be paid," she said.

"No, I didn't. Look. He wears golden rings set with jewels of immense value. Take them, and let's be off."

She shuddered and said, "No. They would

bring misfortune."

"Very well. The next room should be his treasure chamber."

It was. There were chests and boxes filled with emeralds, diamonds, turquoises, rubies, and many other jewels. There were golden and silver idols and statuettes. There was enough wealth to purchase a dozen of the lesser cities of the empire and all their citizens.

But she could only take what she could carry and not be hampered in the leaving.

Exclaiming ecstatics, she reached toward a coffer sparkling with diamonds.

At her touch, the jewels faded and were gone.

She cried out in anguish.

"They're products of his magic!" Smhee said. "Set here to fool thieves. Benna must have taken one of these, though how he got here and then away I've no idea! The jewel did not disappear because the mage was alive and his powers were strong. But I'll wager that not long after the rat carried the jewel off, it disappeared. That's why the searchers found no jewel though they turned the city upside-down and inside-out!"

"There's plenty of other stuff to take!" she said.

"No, too heavy. But he must have put his real jewels somewhere. The next room!"

But there were no other rooms.

"Don't you believe it," Smhee said. He tore down the tapestries and began tapping on the walls, which were of a dense-grained purplish wood erected over the stone. Presently, he said, "Ah!" and he moved his hands swiftly over the area. "Here's a hole in the wood just big enough to admit my little finger. I put my finger in thus, and I pull thus, and thus . . . !"

A section of the wood swung out. Masha got a burning lamp and thrust it into the room beyond. The light fell on ten open chests and twenty open coffers. Jewels sparkled.

They entered.

"Take two handsful," Smhee said. "That's all. We aren't out of here yet."

Masha untied the little bag attached to her belt, hesitated, then scooped out enough to fill the bag. It almost tore her heart apart to leave the rest, but she knew that Smhee's advice was wisdom. Perhaps, some day, she could come back for more. No. That would be stupid. She had far more than enough.

On the way out, Smhee stopped. He opened the mage's robe and revealed a smooth-shaven chest on which was tattooed a representation of a fearful six-armed four-legged being with a glaring long-tusked face. He cut around this and peeled the skin off and put it

rolled and folded into a small jar of ointment.
Replacing the jar in his bag, he rose, saying,
"The goddess knows that I would not lie
about his death. But this will be the proof if
any is demanded."

"Maybe we should look for the mage's
secret exit," she said. "That way, we won't
run into the Raggah."

"No. At any moment someone may see that
the guard is missing. Besides, the mage will
have put traps in his escape route, and we
might not elude those."

They made their way back to the corridor of
the lift shaft without being observed. But two
men stood in front of the entrance to the lift.
They were talking excitedly and looking down
the shaft. Then one ran down the corridor,
away from the corner behind which the two
intruders watched.

"Going to get help before they venture
down to find out why the two feeders haven't
come back," Smhee muttered.

The man who'd stayed was looking down
the shaft. Masha and Smhee took him from
behind, one cutting the throat, the other stabbing him in the back. They let themselves
down on the ropes and then cut them before
going down through the open trapdoor. But
as they left the cage, a spear shot through the
trapdoor and thudded point-first into the
floor. Men shouted above.

"They'll bring ropes and come down on
those," Smhee said. "And they'll send others

outside to catch us when we come out of the pool. Run, but remember the traps!"

And the spiders, she thought. And the crabs. I hope the bears are dead.

They were. The spiders, all real now that the mage was dead, were alive. These were driven back by the torches the two had paused to light, and they got to the skin-boat. They pushed this out and began paddling with desperation. The craft went through the first arch and then through the second. To their right now were some ledges on which were masses of pale-white things with stalked eyes and clacking pincers. The crabs. The two directed their boat away from these, but the writhing masses suddenly became individual figures leaping outward and splashing into the dark water. Very quickly, the ledges were bare. There was no sign of the monsters, but the two knew that these were swimming toward them.

They paddled even faster, though it had not seemed possible until then. And then the prow of the boat bumped into the wall.

"Swim for it!" Smhee bellowed, his voice rebounding from the far walls and high ceilings of the cave.

Masha feared entering the water; she expected to be seized by those huge claws. But she went over, the boat tipping, and dived.

Something did touch her leg as she went under the stone downcropping. Then her head was above the surface of the pool and Smhee's was beside her.

They scrambled out onto the hard stone. Behind them came the clacking, but none of the crabs tried to leave the pool.

The sky was black; thunder bellowed in the north; lightning traced white veins. A wind blew, chilling them in their wet clothes.

They ran toward the dugout but not in a straight line since they had to avoid the bushes with the poisonous thorns. Before they reached it, rain fell. They dragged the craft into the river and got aboard. Above them lightning cracked across the sky. Another bolt struck shortly thereafter, revealing two bears and a number of men behind them.

"They can't catch us now!" Smhee yelled. "But they'll be going back to put their horses on rafts. They'll go all the way into Sanctuary itself to get us!"

Save your breath, Masha thought. I know all that.

The wind-struck river was rough now, but they got through the waves to the opposite shore. They climbed panting up the ridge and found their horses, whinnying from fear of the lightning. When they got to the bottom of the ridge, they sped away, their passage fitfully lit by the dreadful whiteness that seemed to smash all around them. They kept their horses at a gallop for a mile, then ceased them up.

"There's no way they can catch us!" Smhee

shouted through the thunder. "We've got too much of a head-start!"

Dawn came. The rain stopped. The clouds cleared away; the hot winter sun of the desert rose. They stopped at the hut where they had slept, and the horses rested, and they ate bread and cheese.

"Three more hours will bring us within sight of Sanctuary," the fat man said. "We'll get your family aboard the *Swordfish*, and the Raggah can search for us in vain."

He paused, then said, "What do you intend to do about Eevroen?"

"Nothing," she said. "If he gets in my way I'll brain him again."

He laughed so much he choked on his bread. When he'd cleared his throat, he said, "You are some woman! Brave as the goddess makes them! And supple in mind, too! If I were not vowed to chastity, I would woo you! I may be forty-five and fat, but . . . ."

He stopped to stare down at his hand. His face froze into an expression of horror.

Marsha became equally paralyzed.

A small purple spider was on Smhee's hand.

"Move slowly," he said softly through rigid lips. "I dare not move. Slap it when you've got your hand within a few inches of it."

She got up and took a step toward him. Where had the creature come from? There were no webs in the hut. Had it come from outside and crawled upon him?

She took another step, leaned over, and

brought her hand slowly down at an angle toward the thing. Its eyes were black and motionless, seemingly unaware of her presence.

Maybe it's not poisonous, she thought.

Suddenly, Smhee screamed, and he crushed the spider with his other hand. He leaped up then, brushing off the tiny body.

"It bit me! It bit me!"

The dark swelling had started.

"It's not one of the mage's creatures," she said. "Its venom may not be deadly."

"It's the mage's," he said. His face was white under the heavy pigment.

"It must have crawled into my bag. It couldn't have done it when we were on the way to the mage's rooms. It must have gotten in when I opened the bag to skin off the tattoo."

He howled. "The mage has gotten his revenge!"

"You don't know that," she said, but she was certain that it was as Smhee had said. She removed her small belt-bag and carefully poured out the jewels. But that was all it contained.

"It's beginning to hurt," Smhee said. "I can make it back to the city. Benna did, and he was bitten many times. But I know these spiders. I will die as surely as he did, though I will take longer. There is no antidote."

He sat down, and for a while he rocked back and forth, eyes closed, moaning. Then he said,

"Masha, there is no sense in my going on with you. But, since I have made it possible for you to be as wealthy as a queen, I beg you to do one favor for me. If it is not too much to ask."

"What is that?" she said.

"Take the jar containing the tattooed skin to Sherranpip. And there tell our story to the highest priest of Weda Krizhtawn. He will pray for me to her, and a great tombstone will be erected for me in the courtyard of the peacocks, and pilgrims will come from all over Sherranpip and the islands around and will pray for me. But if you don't want . . ."

Masha knelt and kissed him on the mouth. He felt cold.

She stood up and said, "I promise you that I will do that. That, as you said, is the least I can do."

He smiled, though it cost him to do it.

"Good. Then I can die in peace. Go. May Weda Krizhtawn bless you."

"But the Raggah . . . they will torture you!"

"No. This bag contains a small vial of poison. They will find only a corpse. If they find me at all."

Masha burst into tears, but she took the jar, and after kissing Smhee again, she rode off, his horse trotting behind hers.

At the top of the hill she stopped to look behind at the hut.

Far off, coming swiftly, was a dark mass. The Raggah.

She turned away and urged her horse into a gallop.

THE MAKING OF
REVELATION, PART I

God said, "Bring me Cecil B. DeMille."

"Dead or alive?" the angel Gabriel said.

"I want to make him an offer he can't refuse. Can even *I* do this to a dead man?"

"Oh, I see," said Gabriel, who didn't. "It will be done."

And it was.

Cecil Blount DeMille, confused, stood in front of the desk. He didn't like it. He was used to sitting behind the desk while others stood. Considering the circumstances, he wasn't about to protest. The giant, divinely handsome, bearded, pipe-smoking man behind the desk was not one you'd screw around with. However, the gray eyes, though steely, weren't quite those of a Wall Street banker. They held a hint of compassion.

Unable to meet those eyes, DeMille looked at the angel by his side. He'd always thought angels had wings. This one didn't, though he could certainly fly. He'd carried DeMille in his arms up through the stratosphere to a city of gold somewhere between the Earth and the moon. Without a space suit, too.

God, like all great entities, came right to the point.

"This is 1980 A.D. In twenty years it'll be time for The Millennium. The day of judgement. The events as depicted in the Book of Revelation or the Apocalypse by St. John the Divine. You know, the seven seals, the four horsemen, the moon dripping blood, Armageddon, and all that."

DeMille wished he'd be invited to sit down. Being dead for twenty-one years, during which he'd not moved a muscle, had tended to weaken him.

"Take a chair," God said. "Gabe, bring the man a brandy." He puffed on his pipe; tiny lightning crackled through the clouds of smoke.

"Here you are, Mr. DeMille," Gabriel said, handing him the liqueur in a cut quartz goblet. "Napoleon 1880."

DeMille knew there wasn't any such thing as a one-hundred year old brandy, but he didn't argue. Anyway, the stuff certainly tasted like it was. They really lived up here.

God sighed, and he said, "The main trouble is that not many people really believe in Me any more. So My powers are not what they once were. The old gods, Zeus, Odin, all that bunch, lost their strength and just faded away, like old soldiers, when their worshippers ceased to believe in them.

"So, I just can't handle the end of the world by Myself any more. I need someone with experience, know-how, connections, and a reputation. Somebody people know really existed. You. Unless you know of somebody who's made more Biblical epics than you have."

"That'll be the day," DeMille said. "But what about the unions? They really gave me a hard time, the commie bas . . . uh, so-and-so's. Are they as strong as ever?"

"You wouldn't believe their clout nowadays."

DeMille bit his lip, then said, "I want them dissolved. If I only got twenty years to produce this film, I can't be held up by a bunch of goldbrickers."

"No way," God said. "They'd all strike, and we can't afford any delays."

He looked at his big railroad watch. "We're going to be on a very tight schedule."

"Well, I don't know," DeMille said. "You can't get anything done with all their regulations, interunion jealousies, and the featherbedding. And the wages! It's no wonder it's so hard to show a profit. It's too much of a hassle!"

"I can always get D. W. Griffith."

DeMille's face turned red. "You want a

grade-B production? No, no, that's all right!
I'll do it, do it!"

God smiled and leaned back. "I thought so.
By the way, you're not the producer, too; I am.
My angels will be the executive producers.
They haven't had much to do for several mil-
lennia, and the devil makes work for idle
hands, you know. Haw, haw! You'll be the
chief director, of course. But this is going to
be quite a job. You'll have to have at least a
hundred thousand assistant directors."

"But . . . that means training about 99,000
directors!"

"That's the least of our problems. Now you
can see why I want to get things going immediately."

DeMille gripped the arms of the chair and
said, weakly, "Who's going to finance this?"

God frowned. "That's another problem. My
Antagonist has control of all the banks. If
worse comes to worse, I could melt down the
heavenly city and sell it. But the bottom of the
gold market would drop all the way to hell.
And I'd have to move to Beverly Hills. You
wouldn't believe the smog there or the prices
they're asking for houses.

"However, I think I can get the money.
Leave that to Me."

The men who really owned the American
banks sat at a long mahogany table in a huge
room in a Manhattan skyscraper. The Chairman of the Board sat at the head. He didn't

have the horns, tail, and hooves which legend gave him. Nor did he have an odor of brimstone. More like Brut. He was devilishly handsome and the biggest and best-built man in the room. He looked like he could have been the chief of the angels and in fact once had been. His eyes were evil but no more so than the others at the table, bar one.

The exception, Raphael, sat at the other end of the table. The only detractions from his angelic appearance were his bloodshot eyes. His apartment on West Side had paper-thin walls, and the swingers' party next door had kept him awake most of the night. Despite his fatigue, he'd been quite effective in presenting the offer from above.

Don Francisco "The Fixer" Fica drank a sixth glass of wine to up his courage, made the sign of the cross, most offensive to the Chairman, gulped, and spoke.

"I'm sorry, Signor, but that's the way the vote went. One hundred percent. It's a purely business proposition, legal, too, and there's no way we won't make a huge profit from it. We're gonna finance the movie, come hell or high water!"

Satan reared up from his chair and slammed a huge but well-manicured fist onto the table. Glasses of vino crashed over; plates half-filled with pasta and spaghetti rattled. All but Raphael paled.

"Dio motarello! Lecaculi! Cacasotti! Non romperci i coglioni! I'm the Chairman, and I

say no, no, no!"

Fica looked at the other heads of the families. Mignotta, Fregna, Stronza, Loffa, Recchione, and Bocchino seemed scared, but each nodded the go-ahead at Fica.

"I'm indeed sorry that you don't see it our way," Fica said. "But I must ask for your resignation."

Only Raphael could meet The Big One's eyes, but business was business. Satan cursed and threatened. Nevertheless, he was stripped of all his shares of stock. He'd walked in the richest man in the world, and he stormed out penniless and an ex-member of the Organization.

Raphael caught up with him as he strode mumbling up Park Avenue.

"You're the father of lies," Raphael said, "so you can easily be a great success as an actor or politician. There's money in both fields. Fame, too. I suggest acting. You've got more friends in Hollywood than anywhere else."

"Are you nuts?" Satan snarled.

"No. Listen. I'm authorized to sign you up for the film on the end of the world. You'll be a lead, get top billing. You'll have to share it with The Son, but we can guarantee you a bigger dressing room than His. You'll be playing yourself, so it ought to be easy work."

Satan laughed so loudly that he cleared the sidewalks for two blocks. The Empire State Building swayed more than it should have in the wind.

"You and your boss must think I'm pretty dumb! Without me the film's a flop. You're up a creek without a paddle. Why should I help you? If I do I end up at the bottom of a flaming pit forever. Bug off!"

Raphael shouted after him, "We can always get Roman Polanski!"

Raphael reported to God, who was taking His ease on His jasper and cornelian throne above which glowed a rainbow.

"He's right, Your Divinity. If he refuses to cooperate, the whole deal's off. No real Satan, no real Apocalypse."

God smiled. "We'll see."

Raphael wanted to ask Him what He had in mind. But an angel appeared with a request that God come to the special effects department. Its technicians were having trouble with the roll-up-the-sky-like-a-scroll machine.

"Schmucks!" God growled. "Do I have to do everything?"

Satan moved into a tenement on 121st Street and went on welfare. It wasn't a bad life, not for one who was used to Hell. But two months later, his checks quit coming. There was no unemployment any more. Anyone who was capable of working but wouldn't was out of luck. What had happened was that Central Casting had hired everybody in the world as production workers, stars, bit players, or extras.

Meanwhile, all the advertising agencies in the world had spread the word, good or bad depending upon the viewpoint, that the Bible was true. If you weren't a Christian, and, what was worse, a sincere Christian, you were doomed to perdition.

Raphael shot up to Heaven again.

"My God, You wouldn't believe what's happening! The Christians are repenting of their sins and promising to be good forever and ever, amen! The Jews, Moslems, Hindus, Buddhists, scientologists, animists, you name them, are lining up at the baptismal fonts! What a mess! The atheists have converted, too, and all the communist and Marxian socialist governments have been overthrown!"

"That's nice," God said. "But I'll really believe in the sincerity of the Christian nations when they kick out their present administrations. Down to the local dogcatcher."

"They're doing it!" Raphael shouted. "But maybe You don't understand! This isn't the way things go in the *Book of Revelation!* We'll have to do some very extensive rewriting of the script! Unless You straighten things out!"

God seemed very calm. "The script? How's Ellison coming along with it?"

Of course, God knew everything that was happening, but He pretended sometimes that He didn't. It was His excuse for talking. Just issuing a command every once in a while made for long silences, sometimes lasting for centuries.

He had hired only science-fiction writers to

work on the script since they were the only ones with imaginations big enough to handle the job. Besides, they weren't bothered by scientific impossibilities. God loved Ellison, the head writer, because he was the only human he'd met so far who wasn't afraid to argue with Him. Ellison was severely handicapped, however, because he wasn't allowed to use obscenities while in His presence.

"Ellison's going to have a hemorrhage when he finds out about the rewrites," Raphael said. "He gets screaming mad if anyone messes around with his scripts."

"I'll have him up for dinner," God said. "If he gets too obstreperous, I'll toss around a few lightning bolts. If he thinks he was burned before . . . Well!"

Raphael wanted to question God about the tampering with the book, but just then the head of Budgets came in. The angel beat it. God got very upset when He had to deal with money matters.

The head assistant director said, "We got a big problem now, Mr. DeMille. We can't have any Armageddon. Israel's willing to rent the site to us, but where are we going to get the forces of Gog and Magog to fight against the good guys? Everybody's converted. Nobody's willing to fight on the side of anti-Christ and Satan. That means we've got to change the script again. I don't want to be the one to tell Ellison . . ."

"Do I have to think of everything?" DeMille said. "It's no problem: Just hire actors to play the villains."

"I already thought of that. But they want a bonus. They say they might be persecuted just for *playing* the guys in the black hats. They call it the social-stigma bonus. But the guilds and the unions won't go for it. Equal pay for all extras or no movie and that's that."

DeMille sighed. "It won't make any difference anyway as long as we can't get Satan to play himself."

The assistant nodded. So far, they'd been shooting around the devil's scenes. But they couldn't put it off much longer.

DeMille stood up. "I have to watch the auditions for The Great Whore of Babylon."

The field of 100,000 candidates for the role had been narrowed to a hundred, but from what he'd heard none of these could play the part. They were all good Christians now, no matter what they'd been before, and they just didn't have their hearts in the role. DeMille had intended to cast his brand-new mistress, a starlet, a hot little number—if promises meant anything—one hundred percent right for the part. But just before they went to bed for the first time, he'd gotten a phone call.

"None of this hankypanky, C.B.," God had said. "You're now a devout worshipper of Me, one of the lost sheep that's found its way back to the fold. So get with it. Otherwise, back to Forest Lawn for you, and I use Griffith."

"But . . . but I'm Cecil B. DeMille! The rules are O.K. for the common people, but . . ."

"Throw that scarlet woman out! Shape up or ship out! If you marry her, fine! But remember, there'll be no more divorces!"

DeMille was glum. Eternity was going to be like living forever next door to the Board of Censors.

The next day, his secretary, very excited, buzzed him.

"Mr. DeMille! Satan's here! I don't have him for an appointment, but he says he's always had a long-standing one with you!"

Demoniac laughter bellowed through the intercom.

"C.B., my boy! I've changed my mind! I tried out anonymously for the part, but your shithead assistant said I wasn't the type for the role! So I've come to you! I can start work as soon as we sign the contract!"

The contract, however, was not the one the great director had in mind. Satan, smoking a big cigar, chuckling, cavorting, read the terms.

"And don't worry about signing in your blood. It's unsanitary. Just ink in your John Henry, and all's well that ends in Hell."

"You get my soul," DeMille said weakly.

"It's not much of a bargain for me. But if you don't sign it, you won't get me. Without me, the movie's a bomb. Ask The Producer, He'll tell you how it is."

"I'll call Him now."

"No! Sign now, this very second, or I walk out forever!"

DeMille bowed his head, more in pain than in prayer.

"Now!"

DeMille wrote on the dotted line. There had never been any genuine indecision. After all, he was a film director.

After snickering Satan had left, DeMille punched a phone number. The circuits transmitted this to a station which beamed the pulses up to a satellite which transmitted these directly to the heavenly city. Somehow, he got a wrong number. He hung up quickly when Israfel, the angel of death, answered. The second attempt, he got through.

"Your Divinity, I suppose. You know what I just did? It *was* the only way you could get him to play himself. You understand that, don't You?"

"Yes, but if you're thinking of breaking the contract or getting Me to do it for you, forget it. What kind of an image would I have if I did something unethical like that? But not to worry. He can't get his hooks into your soul until I say so."

Not to worry? DeMille thought. I'm the one who's going to Hell, not Him.

"Speaking of hooks, let Me remind you of a clause in your contract with The Studio. If you ever fall from grace, and I'm not talking about that little bimbo you were going to make your mistress, you'll die. The Mafia isn't the only one that puts out a contract. *Capice?"*

DeMille, sweating and cold, hung up. In a sense, he was already in Hell. All his life with no women except for one wife? It was bad enough to have no variety, but what if whoever he married cut him off, like one of his wives—what was her name?—had done?

Moreover, he couldn't get loaded out of his skull even to forget his marital woes. God, though not prohibiting booze in His Book, had said that moderation in strong liquor was required and no excuses. Well, maybe he could drink beer, however disgustingly plebeian that was.

He wasn't even happy with his work now. He just didn't get the respect he had in the old days. When he chewed out the camerapeople, the grips, the gaffers, the actors, they stormed back at him that he didn't have the proper Christian humility, he was too high and mighty, too arrogant. God would get him if he didn't watch his big fucking mouth.

This left him speechless and quivering. He'd always thought, and acted accordingly, that the director, not God, was God. He remembered telling Charlton Heston that when Heston, who after all was only Moses, had thrown a temper tantrum when he'd stepped in a pile of camel shit during the filming of *The Ten Commandments.*

Was there more to the making of the end-of-the-world than appeared on the surface? Had

God seemingly forgiven everybody their sins and lack of faith but was subtly, even insidiously, making everybody pay by suffering? Had He forgiven but not forgotten? Or vice versa?

God marked even the fall of a sparrow, though why the sparrow, a notoriously obnoxious and dirty bird, should be significant in God's eye was beyond DeMille.

He had the uneasy feeling that everything wasn't as simple and as obvious as he'd thought when he'd been untimely ripped from the grave in a sort of Caesarean section and carried off like a nursing baby in Gabriel's arms to the office of The Ultimate Producer.

From the *Playboy* Interview feature, December, 1980.

Playboy: Mr. Satan, why did you decide to play yourself after all?

Satan: Damned if I know.

Playboy: The rumors are that you'll be required to wear clothes in the latter-day scenes but that you steadfastly refuse. Are these rumors true?

Satan: Yes indeed. Everybody knows I never wear clothes except when I want to appear among humans without attracting undue attention. If I wear clothes it'd be unrealistic. It'd be phoney, though God knows there are enough fake things in this movie. The Producer says this is going to be a PG picture, not an X-rated. That's why I walked off the set the other day. My lawyers are negotiating with

The Studio now about this. But you can bet your ass that I won't go back unless things go my way, the right way. After all, I am an artist, and I have my integrity. Tell me, if you had a prong this size, would you hide it?

Playboy: The Chicago cops would arrest me before I got a block from my pad. I don't know, though, if they'd charge me with indecent exposure or being careless with a natural resource.

Satan: They wouldn't dare arrest me. I got too much on the city administration.

Playboy: That's some whopper. But I thought angels were sexless. You are a fallen angel, aren't you?"

Satan: You jerk! What kind of researcher are you? Right there in the Bible, *Genesis* 6:2, it says that the sons of God, that is, the angels, took the daughters of men as wives and had children by them. You think the kids were test tube babies? Also, you dunce, I refer you to *Jude* 7 where it's said that the angels, like the Sodomites, committed fornications and followed unnatural lusts.

Playboy: Whew! That brimstone! There's no need getting so hot under the collar, Mr. Satan. I only converted a few years ago. I haven't had much chance to read the Bible.

Satan: I read the Bible every day. All of it. I'm a speedreader, you know.

Playboy: You read the Bible? (Pause). Hee, hee! Do you read it for the same reason W. C. Fields did when he was dying?

Satan: What's that?
Playboy: Looking for loopholes.

DeMille was in a satellite and supervising the camerapeople while they shot the takes from ten miles up. He didn't like at all the terrific pressure he was working under. There was no chance to shoot every scene three or four times to get the best angle. Or to reshoot if the actors blew their lines. And, oh, sweet Jesus, they were blowing them all over the world!

He mopped his bald head. "I don't care what The Producer says! We have to retake at least a thousand scenes. And we've a million miles of film to go yet!"

They were getting close to the end of the breaking-of-the-seven-seals sequences. The Lamb, played by The Producer's Son, had just broken the sixth seal. The violent worldwide earthquake had gone well. The sun-turning-black-as-a-funeral-pall had been a breeze. But the moon-all-red-as-blood had had some color problems. The rushes looked more like Colonel Sanders' orange juice than hemoglobin. In DeMille's opinion the stars-falling-to-earth-like-figs-shaken-down-by-a-gale scenes had been excellent, visually speaking. But everybody knew that the stars were not little blazing stones set in the sky but were colossal balls of atomic fires each of which was many times bigger than Earth. Even one of them, a million miles from Earth, would destroy it. So where was the credibility factor?

"I don't understand you, boss," DeMille's assistant said. "You didn't worry about credibility when you made *The Ten Commandments*. When Heston, I mean, Moses, parted the Red Sea, it was the fakiest thing I ever saw. It must've made unbelievers out of millions of Christians. But the film was a box-office success."

"It was the dancing girls that brought off the whole thing!" DeMille screamed. "Who cares about all that other bullshit when they can see all those beautiful long-legged snatches twirling their veils!"

His secretary floated from her chair. "I quit, you male chauvinistic pig! So me and my sisters are just snatches to you, you bald-headed cunt?"

His hotline to the heavenly city rang. He picked up the phone.

"Watch your language!" The Producer thundered. "If you step out of line too many times, I'll send you back to the grave! And Satan gets you right then and there!"

Chastened but boiling near the danger point, DeMille got back to business, called Art in Hollywood. The sweep of the satellite around Earth included the sky-vanishing-as-a-scroll-is-rolled-up scenes, where every-mountain-and-island-is-removed-from-its-place. If the script had called for a literal removing, the tectonics problem would have been terrific and perhaps impossible. But in this case the special effects departments only had to simulate the scenes.

Even so, the budget was strained. However,
The Producer, through his unique abilities,
was able to carry these off. Whereas, in the
original script, genuine displacements of
Greenland, England, Ireland, Japan, and
Madagascar had been called for, not to mention thousands of smaller islands, these were
only faked.

"Your Divinity, I have some bad news,"
Raphael said.
The Producer was too busy to indulge in
talking about something He already knew.
Millions of the faithful had backslid and taken
up their old sinful ways. They believed that
since so many events of the apocalypse were
being faked, God must not be capable of
making any really big catastrophes. So, they
didn't have anything to worry about.
The Producer, however, had decided that it
would not only be good to wipe out some of
the wicked but it would strengthen the faithful if they saw that God still had some muscle.
"They'll get the real thing next time," He
said. "But we have to give DeMille time to set
up his cameras at the right places. And we'll
have to have the script rewritten, of course."
Raphael groaned. "Couldn't somebody else
tell Ellison? He'll carry on something awful."
"I'll tell him. You look pretty pooped, Rafe.
You need a little R&R. Take two weeks off.
But don't do it on Earth. Things are going to
be very unsettling there for a while."
Raphael, who had a tender heart, said,

"Thanks, Boss. I'd just as soon not be around to see it."

The seal was stamped on the foreheads of the faithful, marking them safe from the burning of a third of Earth, the turning of a third of the sea to blood along with the sinking of a third of the ships at sea (which also included the crashing of a third of the airplanes in the air, something St. John had overlooked), the turning of a third of all water to wormwood (a superfluous measure since a third was already thoroughly polluted), the failure of a third of daylight, the release of giant mutant locusts from the abyss, and the release of poison-gas-breathing mutant horses, which slew a third of mankind.

DeMille was delighted. Never had such terrifying scenes were filmed. And these were nothing to the plagues which followed. He had enough film from the cutting room to make a hundred documentaries after the movie was shown. And then he got a call from The Producer.

"It's back to the special effects, my boy."

"But why, Your Divinity? We still have to shoot the-Great-Whore-of-Babylon sequences, the two - Beasts - and - the - marking - of - the - wicked, the Mount-Zion-and-The-Lamb-with-His-one-hundred-and-forty-thousand-good-men-who-haven't-defiled-themselves-with-women, the . . ."

"Because there aren't any wicked left by now, you dolt! And not too many of the good, either!"

"That couldn't be helped," DeMille said. "Those gas-breathing, scorpion-tailed horses kind of got out of hand. But we just *have* to have the scenes where the rest of mankind that survives the plagues still doesn't abjure its worship of idols and doesn't repent of its murders, sorcery, fornications, and robberies."

"Rewrite the script."

"Ellison will quite for sure this time."

"That's all right. I already have some hack from Peoria lined up to take his place. And cheaper, too."

DeMille took his outfit, one hundred thousand strong, to the heavenly city. Here they shot the war between Satan and his demons and Michael and his angels. This was not in the chronological sequence as written by St. John. But the logistics problems were so tremendous that it was thought best to film these out of order.

Per the rewritten script, Satan and his host were defeated, but a lot of nonbelligerents were casualties, including DeMille's best cameraperson. Moreover, there was a delay in production when Satan insisted that a stuntperson do the part where he was hurled from heaven to Earth.

"Or use a dummy!" he yelled. "Twenty thousand miles is a hell of a long way to fall! If I'm hurt badly I might not be able to finish the movie!"

The screaming match between the director and Satan took place on the edge of the city.

The Producer, unnoticed, came up behind Satan and kicked him from the city for the second time in their relationship with utter ruin and furious combusion.

Shrieking, "I'll sue! I'll sue!" Satan fell towards the planet below. He made a fine spectacle in his blazing entrance into the atmosphere, but the people on Earth paid it little attention. They were used to fiery portents in the sky. In fact, they were getting fed up with them.

DeMille screamed and danced around and jumped up and down. Only the presence of The Producer kept him from using foul and abusive language.

"We didn't get it on camera! Now we'll have to shoot it over!"

"His contract calls for only one fall," God said. "You'd better shoot the War-between-The-Faithful-and-True-Rider-against-the-beast -and-the-false-prophet while he recovers."

"What'll I do about the fall?" DeMille moaned.

"Fake it," the Producer said, and He went back to His office.

Per the script, an angel came down from heaven and bound up the badly injured and burned and groaning Satan with a chain and threw him into the abyss, the Grand Canyon. Then he shut and sealed it over him (what a terrific sequence that was!) so that Satan might seduce the nations no more until a thousand years had passed.

A few years later the devil's writhings caused a volcano to form above him, and the Environmental Protection Agency filed suit against Celestial Productions, Inc. because of the resultant pollution of the atmosphere.

Then God, very powerful now that only believers existed on Earth, performed the first resurrection. In this, only the martyrs were raised. And Earth, which had had much elbow room because of the recent wars and plagues, was suddenly crowded again.

Part I was finished except for the reshooting of some scenes, the dubbing in of voice and background noise, and the synchronization of the music, which was done by the cherubim and seraphim (all now unionized).

The great night of the premiere in a newly built theater in Hollywood, six million capacity, arrived. DeMille got a standing ovation after it was over. But *Time* and *Newsweek* and *The Manchester Guardian* panned the movie.

"There are some people who may go to hell after all," God growled.

DeMille didn't care about that. The film was a box-office success, grossing ten billion dollars in the first six months. And when he considered the reruns in theaters and the TV rights . . . well, had anyone ever done better?

He had a thousand more years to live. That seemed like a long time. Now. But . . . what would happen to him when Satan was released to seduce the nations again? According to John the Divine's book, there'd be another worldwide battle. Then Satan, defeated, would be cast into the lake of fire and sulphur in the abyss.

(He'd be allowed to keep his Oscar, however.)

Would God let Satan, per the contract DeMille had signed with the devil, take DeMille with him into the abyss? Or would He keep him safe long enough to finish directing Part II? After Satan was buried for good, there'd be a second resurrection and a judging of those raised from the dead. The goats, the bad guys, would be hurled into the pit to keep Satan company. DeMille should be with the saved, the sheep, because he had been born again. But there was that contract with The Tempter.

DeMille arranged a conference with The Producer. Ostensibly, it was about Part II, but DeMille managed to bring up the subject which really interested him.

"I can't break your contract with him," God said.

"But I only signed it so that You'd be sure to get Satan for the role. It was a self-sacrifice. Greater love hath no man and all that. Doesn't that count for anything?"

"Let's discuss the shooting of the new heaven and the new earth sequences."

At least I'm not going to be put into hell until the movie is done, DeMille thought. But after that? He couldn't endure thinking about it.

"It's going to be a terrible technical

problem," God said, interrupting DeMille's gloomy thoughts. "When the second resurrection takes place, there won't be even Standing Room Only on Earth. That's why I'm dissolving the old earth and making a new one. But I can't just duplicate the old Earth. The problem of Lebensraum would still remain. Now, what I'm contemplating is a Dyson sphere."

"What's that?"

"A scheme by a 20th-century mathematician to break up the giant planet Jupiter into large pieces and set them in orbit at the distance of Earth from the sun. The surfaces of the pieces would provide room for a population enormously larger than Earth's. It's a Godlike concept."

"What a documentary its filming would be!" DeMille said. "Of course, if we could write some love interest in it, we could make a he . . . pardon me, a heaven of a good story!"

God looked at his big railroad watch.

"I have another appointment, C.B. The conference is over."

DeMille said goodby and walked dejectedly towards the door. He still hadn't gotten an answer about his ultimate fate. God was stringing him along. He felt that he wouldn't know until the last minute what was going to happen to him. He'd be suffering a thousand years of uncertainty, of mental torture. His life would be a cliff-hanger. Will God relent? Or will He save the hero at the very last second?

"C.B.," God said.

DeMille spun around, his heart thudding, his knees turned to water. Was this it? The fatal finale? Had God, in His mysterious and subtle way, decided for some reason that there'd be no Continued In Next Chapter for him? It didn't seem likely, but then The Producer had never promised that He'd use him as the director of Part II nor had He signed a contract with him. Maybe, like so many temperamental producers, He'd suddenly concluded that DeMille wasn't the right one for the job. Which meant that He could arrange it so that his ex-director would be thrown now, right this minute, into the lake of fire.

God said, "I can't break your contract with Satan. So . . ."

"Yes?"

DeMille's voice sounded to him as if he were speaking very far away.

"Satan can't have your soul until you die."

"Yes?"

His voice was only a trickle of sound, a last few drops of water from a clogged drainpipe.

"So, if you don't die, and that, of course, depends upon your behavior, Satan can't ever have your soul."

God smiled and said, "See you in eternity."

THE LONG WET
PURPLE DREAM OF
RIP VAN WINKLE

Washington Irving did not know it. Rip did not dare tell it.

Rip hadn't been asleep every day of those twenty years. At least, he didn't think he had. Sometimes he wondered if the reality had just been pleasant, indeed, ecstatic, dreams mixed with nightmares.

In A.D. 1772, Rip was thirty-five when he passed out from the booze snitched from the strange little men playing ninepins. When he awoke on the Kaatskill meadow, his whiskers were no longer than if a night had passed. The bowlers and his dog Wolf were gone. Wincing at every step because of his hangover, he reluctantly trudged over the hills, his hunting

musket on his shoulder, headed for the
Hudson river and home. And the hell his wife
would give him.

Suddenly, he reeled, and he cried out. The
world had become all flux and also fogged
with a very pale purple haze which did not ob-
scure other colors. The leaves of the trees
changed from green to many colors. Autumn
fell like a dead bird and then snow dived after
it. He was up to his waist in it, but he couldn't
feel it. The snow melted. And snow fell again
and again. The rains came; the land greened.
The sun, the moon, and the stars raced across
the sky.

Once a falling tree hurtled *through* him.
Then it decayed and was gone while he yelled
with terror and for mercy. He'd been be-
witched by the little bowlers and justly so. He
should've stayed home, repaired the fences
and house, tilled and planted instead of lazing
around, hunting, and thinking of forbidden
cunt.

Suddenly, the purple haze was gone. The
moon slowed and soon resumed its normal
pace. All was stable again. The hot summer
night was noisy with insects and a great humming from the east. Trembling, he resumed
his trip home. Presently, he stopped on a hill
which looked down on the river, sparkling in
the full moon. The narrow dirt road along the
Hudson was now a broad highway of some
kind of stone. It was brightly illuminated by
lights at the tops of poles along it and by

lamps in the fronts of . . . *horseless carriages?*
The humming was the sound they made when
heard from a distance, and they were going
incredibly fast.

To his right, on top of an empty hill he'd
passed yesterday, was a big house with many
lights and people on the front porch and a
very strange music emanating from it.

Rip went down the hill slowly and quietly.
He was determined to get, somehow, through
all these frightening witcheries to his village,
where the holy presence of the church building would make them all disappear. But he
stopped at the foot of the hill. Parked in a
grove of trees was one of those scary vehicles,
a topless one. Its lights were out. He crept
forward until he saw by the moon that a
woman was sitting in the back seat. She was
smoking tobacco in a little white tube. He
could hear an unfamiliar but stirring music,
then someone shouting, "Hiyo, Silver! Away!"

Closer, he found that the sounds came
from a box in the front part of the carriage.

He looked down past the woman's right
shoulder. Her skirt was up over her waist,
and her hand was working up and down
slowly inside some very thin lacy garments
covering her loins. Her thighs gleamed
whitely between the tops of her stockings—
silk!—and the lacy garment. Her head was
thrown back, the glowing tube sticking
straight up, and she was moaning.

Rip was very embarrassed, but his tally-

whacker was rising. Dame van Winkle had cut
him off after the birth of their eighth; it'd
been a long time since he'd gone to bed with
her. Or anyone.

Rip turned to retreat, and his musket stock
banged against the metal door. The woman
screamed. He started to run away, but his
ankle turned, and he fell flat on his face. The
next he knew, something cold and hard was
pressed against his neck. He looked up at the
woman. She was very pretty, big-busted, and
enticing in that short shameless tight dress.
The huge strange-looking pistol she held was
not so alluring.

She spat out invective with a vigor matched
only by Mrs. van Winkle, who, however,
would never have used such dirty words or
blasphemous oaths. Then she let him get to
his feet.

Eyes wide, she said, "What kind of crazy
outfit is that? Are you a butler from that
house?" Then, seeing the musket, she cried,
"What in hell is that?"

He tried to explain. When she'd heard him
out, she said, "Your name is *Rip van Winkle?*
Now I know you're a refugee from the funny
farm."

"There's no farmer around here by that
name," he said, "unless you mean Klaus van
Fannij."

She looked at the tiny watch on her wrist.
"Shit! Isn't he ever coming back? I get so goddam fed up waiting around for him while he's

sneaking around spying on those big-shot crooks!"

She backed up to the car, reached behind to the rear seat, and brought up a silver flask. She unscrewed the cap of the flask with a thumb, and, still pointing the enormous weapon at him, drank deeply. He smelled gin.

"Here. Have a snort."

He took it gratefully. It *was* gin but terrible stuff. Still, it helped get rid of the shakes, and it warmed the cockles of his heart, not to mention those of his tallywhacker. She saw the expanding bulge; the barrel of her gun dropped as his barrel ascended.

She took the flask back, drained it, then looked at her timepiece again. "Well, why not? It'll serve him right," she said, her words slightly blurred. "Okay. Kneebritches. Off with them."

"My God!" she said as they climbed into the back seat. "It must be at least fourteen inches long!"

"Why, that's only normal," he said. "You should see Brom Dutcher's!"

She laughed and said, "Did you fall asleep and wake up in the twentieth century, Rip?"

He didn't know what she was talking about and didn't much care. After the second time, she offered him a tube which she called a Lucky Strike. He smoked it, but the paper came off on his lip and the tobacco tasted vile.

"I suppose," she said, "you think I'm promiscuous. You know, fucking a complete stranger."

He blushed. Such language from a woman!

"That looney son of a bitch runs around at night in his black hat and cloak, cackling, sneaking around, just itching to blast crooks with his two big .45 automatics. He's knocked off a lot of them, you know." (Rip didn't know.) "I suppose he does much good, socially speaking. But he sure doesn't do me any good. Won't give me a tumble though I practically rub his nose in it. He's not a fairy, so I figure he's either asexual or he thinks his profession, rubbing out gangsters, is holy, just like a priest's, and he's vowed to chastity, too.

"Cranston uses me to spy for him, but he won't let me go with him when he expects some real action. He says it's not women's work, the asshole!"

"Don't he know you're doing this behind his back?" Rip said as he started plugging again.

"He should. He claims to be the only one in the world who knows what evil lurks in the hearts of men. And of women, too. Oh, wow! Oh, God! Pour it in, Kneebritches!"

Maniacal laughter, shuddery and sinister, burst from the shadows. Rip sprang up, dived over the door, jetting, landed on the ground, got up, and began to pull his britches on. The woman, muttering curses, sat up and smoothed her skirt down. A tall man, lean, hawk-faced, with a huge curving nose and wild burning eyes, appeared out of the darkness. He was dressed in strange clothes and carried a bundle under one arm. Rip supposed that was the hat and cloak the woman had mentioned.

"Margo, what do we have here?" the man said. Suddenly, a gun like the woman's was in his long pale hand.

"Some nut who claims to be Rip van Winkle, Lamont."

"I've stirred up a hornet's nest back there. They'll be on our necks in a minute. Let's go!"

Rip said, "Could you drop me off at my village? It's just down the road a mile or so."

The man waved the gun. "Get in the car. You're going to the city with us. I think you're a part of the plot, though I'll admit I don't exactly know how you fit in."

"Oh, Lamont!" the woman said. "Don't be so fucking paranoid! He's been to a masquerade party or he escaped from the puzzle factory or he *is* a time traveler!"

"You've been reading too much of that trashy science fiction. No. He's going with us. I'm getting to the bottom of this if it kills him."

Rip prayed as he held on to the side of the door and Margo's thigh. He was traveling at a speed the philosophers had said no human being could endure. The air rushing over the glass shield in front of him smote him. The lights of the oncoming traffic were blinding.

The nightmare voyage got worse every second. Then they were crossing a gigantic steel bridge over the Hudson. Manhattan was

before him, but the island, which had been
nothing but woods here, was packed with incredibly high buildings and more people in a
mile's stretch than he'd seen in all his life
before.

And then the purple flickering started
again, the sun, moon, stars whirling, snowfall
followed by rain by hot sunlight, flicker,
flicker, flicker. When it stopped, he was
sitting on the same street in bright day, his
ass hurting where he'd fallen through the car,
metal squealing, horns blasting, cursings, and
the front of a car just touching his back. He
had a vague impression he'd been there for a
long time while countless hordes of cars had
passed through his body. But these were
solid, and if he didn't get to the sidewalk fast,
he was going to be run over or badly beaten by
the red-faced driver waving a fist at him.

When he got to the walk, he looked around.
Some of the buildings he'd seen from the
crazy man's car were gone, replaced by others
even taller. At that moment a car pulled up to
the curb near him. It was rusty and dirty with
PEACE and LOVE in big letters painted on it.
What Margo had called a "radio" during the
mad journey to the city was blasting out some
wild barbaric rhythms.

A young woman with a mass of frizzy
yellow hair stuck her head out of its window.
"Hey, man! Far out!"

The driver was a long-haired, bushy-
bearded youth wearing fringed buckskin

clothes and a leather headband. He looked like a frontiersman, an Indian fighter. The female and male in the back seat wore some kind of robes with many bright symbols woven on them. One wore on the chest a round metal object sporting the slogan: *McGovern in '72.* The slogan on the chest ornament of the other was: MAKE LOVE NOT WAR.

The driver said, "Hey, man, I dig those crazy threads. You going to the demonstration?"

Rip thought he might as well say he was. He needed some friendly people to guide him in his stay in this age. Oh, Lord, propelled two hundred years into the future without a return ticket!

Rip got into the front beside the girl, who introduced herself as Judy Gardenier. She asked him if he was going as the "Spirit of 1776." He said he didn't know what she was talking about. As the car headed east on a street that hadn't existed in his time, the three passed a burning tube around. It wasn't white like Margo's Lucky Strike but brown. Its smoke had a heavy acrid odor. Judy asked him if he'd like to try the joint, and he said, "Why not?" Watching him, she said, "Man, you from the sticks? You gotta draw it way down into your lungs and hold it as long as you can."

He did so, and after a few times he began to relax. Things didn't seem so bad now.

"You got any bread?" Judy said.

"Not a bite," Rip said, and the others howled with laughter. When he found out what she meant, he produced from his pocket his worldly wealth, two copper halfpence coins. Judy looked at the King George III heads and the dates, and said, "Wow, collector's items!"

Rip let Judy keep the coins. What the hell.

The trip toward the "pad" in "Hell's Kitchen" was fascinating if sometimes shocking and always confusing. He was startled when he saw the first black and white couple walking along, the man feeling up the woman's ass. The attitude toward slaves certainly had changed. Or did the colonists now have white slaves, too? Whatever the situation was, the color barrier was down.

Women's skirts were, however, up, way up. After he got over his first shock at seeing so much leg, he reveled in it. Nobody else seemed to think such exposure was sinful, so why should he?

The "pad" was in a basement occupied by ten or twelve youths of two or three sexes. A very short stout man with a long red beard, Yosemite Sam, seemed to be the leader.

A girl whose thin blouse obviously had nothing under it, said, "You gotta be putting me on! Rip van Winkle!"

"It's a fake name, of course," Judy said. "Rip, if you're on the run from the pigs, you're safe here. Unless there's a raid."

The four-room apartment was in bad shape, paint peeling, plaster falling, holes in the ceilings, and the furniture looked as if it had been second-hand before Noah's flood.

Everybody seemed to be having a good time, though there were some fierce cries about giving it to the fascist motherfuckers. He puffed a joint being passed around, and then an emaciated girl with huge glazed eyes asked him if he wanted some coke to snort. He said, "Yes," but when she gave him a slip of paper containing some white stuff, he sneezed, and the powder blew all over the girl. She yelled, "That'll be twenty dollars, Sneezy! The only thing I give away is my ass!"

Judy called the girl a freaking ripoff, and the next he knew Judy had thrown her out bodily. While this was going on, Rip told Yosemite Sam that he had to make water. Sam sent him to the place of convenience. But in which bowl was he supposed to urinate? The one on the floor was leaking from the base and had a big turd floating on it. Maybe it was reserved for crap only.

He retraced his steps to Sam and got him aside.

"You mean where you come from you don't have indoor plumbing? I'll bet you don't even have television!"

Rip confessed he'd never heard of either.

Mr. Sam bellowed, "Hey, everybody! Here's a dude so underprivileged you won't believe it! Gather around, folks, and hear him tell it like it is!''

Rip was very embarrassed. Besides, his bladder was hurting. ''I'll be back,'' he muttered, and he tore loose from Sam's grip and pushed his way through to the bathroom. Still lacking instructions, he used the bowl with the pipes, one marked H, the other C. When he turned the handles, both gave cold water.

On the way back to the front room, he came to a stack of wooden crates holding books. Most had paper covers, something unfamiliar to him. The titles were strange: *The Story of O, Red Power, The World of Drugs, I Was A Black Panther for the FBI, The Mother Earth Catalog, The Annotated Fart, Lord of the Rings, Zen Archery, Love and Orgasm.*

A couple near him was arguing about UFOs, and he left the bookcase to get near enough to hear them clearly. But Judy Gardenier pulled him back to the cases, removed a volume, and showed it to him. *The Sketch Book of Geoffrey Crayon, Gent.* by Washington Irving. She opened it to a story titled— amazing—''Rip Van Winkle.''

''Here. Read about your namesake.''

He sat down, his back against the wall, and he slowly lip-read through the tale.

When he was done, he gazed at the wall. He couldn't believe it, but it had to be true. Irving hadn't said anything about his time-traveling. Apparently, he knew nothing about it. Irving said that he'd slept for twenty years and woke up as an old long-bearded man.

Something that especially disturbed him was that his daughter Judith had married a man named Gardenier.

Judy staggered down the hall and sat down by him.

"Kinda makes you freak out, don't it?"

"You mean that you might be my I-don't-know-how-many-times-great-granddaughter?"

"You really like to put a person on, don't you? Nah. I mean the coincidence, the names. Me Judy Gardenier and you Rip van Winkle. He *was* a fictional character, wasn't he? Even if he was real, you couldn't be him. Could you?"

"Just now I don't know who I am."

"That's right. Be cool, baby. The fuzz really after you? No matter, never mind, as Mary Baker Eddy said. Meanwhile, we're all looking for an identity."

She wanted to take him back to the front room where he could tell how he'd been disadvantaged, downtrodden, oppressed, and persecuted. Rip agreed that he'd been all that. But he didn't tell her that it wasn't the capitalist-pig class that'd been doing it to him. It was his wife. And he really couldn't blame her for hen-pecking him. He *had* been a lazy shiftless good-for-nothing who only wanted to hunt and to lounge around in front of van Vedder's tavern.

He said, "Judy, I have to ease myself again. This beer . . . what's in it? . . . I used to be able to drink a gallon before I had to go behind a tree."

He went into the bathroom and pissed in the bowl with the two pipes, idly observing that four more turds had been added to the leaking bowl. He was wondering when the honey-dipper men would come to carry the crap away when the door opened and a woman came in.

He started to protest. She screamed and ran out of the room. A minute later, two men burst in as if they expected to find a wild Indian there. They looked at Rip and started laughing. Before he could make himself decent, they seized him and carried him down the hall to the front room.

"Hey, everybody, look at this!" one of the men shouted. "This is the club Annie thought he was going to hit her with!"

The two let Rip down, and he stuffed his pisseroo into his britches and buttoned his fly. He was both embarrassed and flattered by the raucous remarks of the crowd.

The party went on and on, far past midnight. Rip wasn't used to staying awake much after dusk, but excitement kept him going. Finally, after almost everybody else had left the pad or passed out, Rip found a place behind a sofa and hurtled into sleep.

Since he was as drunk as Davy's sow, his cock should have been snakeshit-limp. He awoke, however, with his maiden's delight as hard as a tax-collector's heart, rising heavenward like the Tower of Babel, expanding like the British Empire. In the dim light he saw Judy, naked, crouching by him, his whacker in her hand. She certainly wasn't bobbing for apples.

Rip had always thought that this sinful act would disgust him, but it didn't. Far from it.

Judy stopped it, looked at the pulsing monolith in her hand, shrieked, and then crawled on top of him. His bumper slid into her greasy cunny as easily as a money-bag into a politician's pocket. She clamped her bunny muscle around his flailer, and they were off on the roller coaster, boxing the long compass, Eve riding Adam's tail. They came together, yelling as if the room was on fire.

After breakfast, Judy said, "The demonstration is this afternoon. This morning I'll start proceedings to get you on welfare."

She had to explain this. He was amazed. "You mean I get paid for not working?"

Judy, hearing this, laughed and said, "Rip, you're a natural-born hippie."

But his visions of paradise vanished when Judy found that he had no social security card, no ID of any kind.

"I don't know," Judy said. "Those clothes, the 1772 coins, your ignorance . . . you couldn't *really* be Rip van Winkle, could you?"

"Would you believe me if I said I was?"

"Not unless I was on something. Never mind. I'll get you a card, and you can apply.

Meanwhile, how about taking a shower with me? I sold your halfpence this morning and bought some pot with part of the bread, but I used to rest of it to pay a plumber to fix up the toilet and shower."

Rip was agreeable since it seemed to him that there was more involved than just washing dirt off. He was right. This age was heaven, even if it was flawed. But then he was no perfectionist.

That afternoon he boarded a rusty old bus with about fifty others. It broke down a mile from where the parade started, and they walked the rest of the way. Rip carried a placard: DICK US NO DICKS. Judy carried: NO MORE BLOODSHED IN VIETNAM. He didn't know what the signs meant and didn't want to be ridiculed if he showed his ignorance. But it was all exciting. More had happened to him in one day than in all his life in his sleepy little village.

While he was marching along, the band playing, and he was shouting the slogans he heard the others cry out and giving the V sign, which he supposed meant, "Up yours," a beautiful redhead with huge conical tits grabbed his crotch.

"How're they, Pops? They say you're tops. You got a dong like King Kong; more jism than bishops have chrism."

Rip grinned. He felt as happy as a favorite nephew whose rich uncle has just died, as ecstatic as a stutterer who's just had a good vowel movement. So he usually didn't know what people were talking about or what was going on most of the time? Most of the people he'd met didn't know either, since they were stoned most of the time. And so the food and liquor tasted like someone had farted in them? He could acquire a taste for them.

Suddenly, there was a lot of yelling and screaming, whistles blowing, and he was running for no reason except that everybody else was, and he was laughing like a woodpecker that'd hammered its brains out drilling for bugs in a streetlamp post. Maybe he might get his head busted or get thrown into gaol, but it was worth it. Such fun!

He threw his placard down just before summer fell away like a politician's virtue at the first bribe offered. The light purple haze swirled. Snow he couldn't feel sifted through him. Nights and days blinked like a whore batting her eyes at him. The seasons whirled around like a brindled dog chasing its tail.

"Oh, no! Not again!"

As suddenly as it had started, the gallop of time ceased. He was on the same spot and in the blaze of summer. People elbowed and jostled and groped him, but they were not those he'd left in the 70's. However, something unusual was going on. A parade of some sort. Here came a band, followed by a float bearing a huge animal figure, a funny-looking elephant, and then a group of fat elderly men dressed like Algerian pirates. Fezes, baggy pants, fake scimitars. Their leader carried a sign:

SHRINERS FOR LEX N. ORDO
AGAINST ANTI-LIFE MURDERERS

At the rear was a man dressed like the Sultan of Turkey. His sign said:

ONE FAMILY, ONE HEAD, ONE VOTE

Behind him came marching women in white semi-military uniforms and veils. Many carried infants in their arms or jerked along toddlers. Their leader's sign said:

CHURCH, CHOW, CHILDREN

A very pregnant young woman, wearing gloves despite the heat, bumped against Rip. She snarled at him; he backed away. He glimpsed the butt of a handgun in her open handbag.

Aimlessly, he made his way through the spectators thronged along the street. It seemed to him that he'd never seen so many knocked-up women in one place. All were gloved. Was there a new custom that pregnant females had to cover their hands when in public?

He approached a very young woman, big like so many nowadays, a head taller than he. Her size wasn't her only elephantine feature.

Her belly looked like she'd been carrying the baby for eighteen months.

He mumbled, "I been kind of out of things for some time. What year is this?"

She stared at him, then laughed.

"You a wino? Or you been in the slammer? It's 1987, shithead. It's also the year of the greatest infamy in history! The blackest, the lowest, the most degrading, the Naziest! That self-righteous puritanical motherfucking male-pig-chauvinist tight-assed fascist Ordo!"

"What? Who?" Rip said, trying to back away but stopped by the crowd.

"You must of been in solitary confinement! Or are you an acidhead? The President, you twit-brained prickface! That's who! He finally got the anti-abortion amendment passed! So . . . look at me! You can't even find a back-room butcher nowadays! They're scared they'll be sent up for life, and . . ."

"Here he comes!" someone shouted, and the cheering and clapping drowned out whatever else she was saying. The people were jumping up and down like barefooted sinners in hell and weeping tears bigger than horse apples. Nearby, a man, mouth frothing, eyes rolling, was down on the pavement trying to bite chunks out of the curbing. If no one else loved him, his dentist did.

First came six cars crowded with grim-faced men carrying rifles. Then a bunch of motorcycle cops. Then some armed toughs running ahead of a topless car. In its front

seat were a driver and two men with set faces
but nervous eyes and, in the back, a good-
looking but aged woman and a man standing
up and waving and grinning like an opium-
smoker who'd just had a successful session in
a comfort station.

The roar of the crowd pressed in on Rip like
a bill-collector who's finally cornered his victim. It wasn't so loud, though, that it covered
the almost simultaneous explosions of fifty—
a hundred?—handguns. The big woman's
pistol went off an inch from Rip's ear, causing
him to crap in his pants. A second later, the
gun flew high over him and landed in the
street.

Rip whirled. Though deafened, he could
read the woman's lips.

"There! Let the shitheads try to figure out
who shot the asshole!"

Was it a conspiracy? Could a hundred
women, or men, for that matter, keep a plot
like that to themselves? Hell, no. A hundred
pregnant women had just happened to come
here with the same idea. Who knew how many
more were further down the street, waiting
for the chance they'd never get?

Now the guns were flying everywhere, like
steel semen from a jacked-off robot. Their
owners were getting rid of them and shucking
their gloves, too. Their target was lying in the
street, pumping blood from at least fifty
holes. If he'd been an oil field, America could
have told OPEC to fuck off.

Once more, Rip was running. The dead man's guards were firing everywhere, and innocent bystanders, some not so innocent, were dropping like fleas from a poisoned dog. Rip finally got clear of the massacre, though he was twice trampled, kicked in the balls once, and clawed so many times he lost most of his clothes and much of his skin. He was reminded of the one time he'd tallywhacked Brom Dutcher's wife. But now he wasn't getting any pleasure whatsoever.

He ran into a tavern. Panting, he stood by the window and watched the noisy turmoil outside. Then, hearing a small thunderous noise, he turned. Cold ran over him. The noise had been too much like that of the game of ninepins the little old men had played while he drank their Hollands gin, so excellent in taste but so surprising in its effects. He saw some bowling alleys, something new to him. But he paid them no attention. Facing him were two of the little old men. One was the commander, the stout old gentleman in the laced doublet, high-crowned hat, red stockings, and high-heeled shoes.

He spoke in a foreign accent. "It took us some time to track you through time, Rip. Too much of the elixir does more than put you into suspended animation. Anyway, let's go."

"No, no!" Rip said loudly, hoping the patrons would come to his rescue. "Please! This age isn't paradise, but . . ."

This wasn't old New York where every-

body's business was yours. No one wanted to
get involved now. While the patrons turned
away or just watched, the other little man
jabbed something into Rip's arm. Uncon-
sciousness fell on him like a mugger.

Just as in the book he'd read, he awoke in
A.D. 1792, in the same place where he'd
fallen asleep. He had a backache ten times
worse than all his hangovers put together. It
wasn't from all the fucking he'd done. You
couldn't lie on your back without moving for
twenty years and not get a backache. Fortunately, the elixir had somehow kept him from
freezing to death and had prevented bedsores.

Trudging down to the village, weeping for
his lost if half-assed Eden, he thought about
the little men. Unlike Washington Irving, Rip
didn't think they were the spirits of Henry
Hudson and his crew. They were men from
outer space, maybe from one of those UFOs
that couple had talked about. Or time
travelers from the far future.

When Rip got to the village, he knew how to
act. Hadn't the scenario been written for him,
wouldn't it *be*, rather, by that hack Irving
forty-seven years from now? But life wasn't
too bad, as it turned out. He was an old man
now, fifty-five, and nobody expected him to
work for a living. Come to think of it, none but
his now departed wife had ever expected it of
him. His daughter's husband, a genial fellow,
didn't mind supporting him, especially since
Rip was now a living legend.

Rip sat often in front of Doolittle's Union Hotel, which had once been van Vedder's Tavern, and he told the story as Irving had, and he got so many free drinks he almost couldn't handle them.

Sometimes, late in the afternoon, loaded with more booze than a rumrunner's ship, he'd close his eyes and doze or seem to doze. The loafers and the tourists around him would see his face clench in fright. They figured he was having a nightmare, and they were right. He was thinking about the bad things in the 20th century, and those would give even the natives of that time nightmares.

Other times, he'd smile, his hips would rotate, and his beard would rise where it covered his fly. Chuckling, snorting, nudging each other's ribs with their elbows, they'd figure that old horny Rip was having a wet dream. They were right, but they didn't know how purple it was.